Blind Fury

VIBE a Steamy Romance

Series #4

Blind Fury

Lynn Chantale

4 Horsemen
Publications, Inc.

4 Horsemen
Publications, Inc.

4 Horsemen Publications, Inc.
1497 Main St. Suite 169
Dunedin, FL 34698
4horsemenpublications.com
info@4horsemenpublications.com

Cover by 4 Horsemen Publications, Inc.
Typesetting by Autumn Skye
Edited by Muñeca Fossette

Library of Congress Control Number: 2022933958

Epub ISBN 978-1-64450-578-6
Audio ISBN 978-1-64450-577-9
Print ISBN 978-1-64450-579-3

Dedication

There are always many people to thank and acknowledge; you know who you are. Thank you!

Table of Contents

Prologue

The damn dog wouldn't stop whining. Samson Denver pulled the pillow over his head in a vain attempt to shut out the insistent yapping. Any other day he could tolerate the little bitch and her noise. Today was not that day.

Yip-Yip-Yip.

Samson groaned. Why did people insist on having pets if they would keep them in a cage 23 hours a day? He could also smell the odor of dog feces and urine permeating his room.

"Shut. Up!" he roared.

For a moment, the dog was quiet.

Samson could now hear his pulse throbbing in his ears and a passing vehicle on the slick street outside his window. He opened his eyes to darkness. His gaze darted around the room, searching for any hint of light. He closed his eyes again to more darkness.

Anger and despair festered, roiled, and set his teeth on edge. One stupid mistake. Not even his mistake. It was some idiot playing around, and now he was condemned to darkness.

The career he'd carefully crafted and built was gone in a flash. *Or rather a bang*, he thought with black humor.

At least he could escape into the sweet oblivion of sleep. As long as he made it to PT and the other appointments, his family left him alone.

Alone. He needed to get used to that. What woman would want him now?

The bright flash of a smile on a curvy, brown-skinned woman flirted in his mind's eye for a moment. She had a beautiful soprano voice. And he'd gone a couple of dates before.

Samson flopped to his back, letting the pillow rest over his face. Could he hold the material there until he passed out? Could he suffocate himself?

He didn't know how others faced the darkness day in and day out. How could they function without ever seeing a rainbow? A loved one's face? Or even their own? What about driving? No more riding his Harley.

And the music...

Yip-Yip-Yip

That's it. Samson had had enough. For weeks, he'd listened to the little bitch whine, yap, and bark at every creak, crack, and whistle. He didn't need sight to do his family a great service by finally taking care of the little ankle biter.

Samson nearly fell from the bed in his haste to stand. He flung out a hand; his fingers met the louvered panes of the closet. He jerked open the door with such force it came off the track.

He didn't care.

Hangers scratched across the metal rod as Samson shoved clothes aside to reach the wall safe at the back of the closet. Thankfully, he didn't need to worry about a combination. He couldn't see the blasted numbers anymore anyway. He pressed his thumb to the pad and heard a click.

He patted the inside of the safe until his fingers curled around a familiar weapon. He didn't need his eyes to check if there was a round chambered. There was.

His family thought they'd removed all his weapons. But his family didn't know about this safe. After all, this was his house. His room. And he always kept weapons. After all, he was a cop.

Had been a cop, he thought bitterly.

If only that damn dog would stop barking!

That's okay. Let the dog keep barking. Samson lifted the gun. He would give that damn dog something to bark about.

Chapter One

One Year Ago

He knew that voice! Samson "Stx" Denver moved closer to the stage. The woman singing was wearing dark leggings, a bright tunic top in a shade between electric blue and turquoise, and a matching scarf that held her long sisterlocks away from her face.

Samson's heart skipped a beat. August River was here. She was the first girl he ever said "I love you" to, the girl he'd lost his virginity to. He smiled at the memory. Both of them were inexperienced first timers, but it had been the best experience of his young life. Sure, there had been some fumbling, but he took his time to avoid rushing through their first time. He still dreamed about it. Would she remember their first time, or had she completely forgotten him?

Samson studied her. He'd never forgotten her. How long had it been since they'd seen one another? Ten? Maybe fifteen years? She'd been married then. And before that, she'd broken his heart. Or was it the other way around?

Either way, they hadn't lasted past high school. And here she was at the monthly social for the Council for the

Blind. He'd known that she'd had a degenerative eye condition that could lead to total blindness. She was one of the reasons he was involved with the Council. And now she was here.

He maneuvered closer to the steps so he would be in a position to be one of the first well-wishers to greet her when she came down.

While Samson watched and listened to August, he realized why none of his relationships lasted. Part of the reason was his career choice, but the rest was that he had been subconsciously searching for another August. But no other woman could meet the standard. One or two had come close, but the women always lacked that special spark. Without that spark, Samson didn't want them.

Now he had a second chance to make August his. He had heard that she was divorced and moved back to Michigan. He returned his attention to the stage where August was going into the bridge for "A Long Walk." Her breath control was amazing, and she made it seem effortless.

Samson glanced around the bar. The crowd was totally into August, swaying to the beat, clapping, and calling encouragement. Whatever had transpired in the past, Samson was happy to see she was still singing.

August bowed at the uproarious applause and blew the audience a kiss as the last note trailed off. Samson laughed at this. A man of medium height wearing a polo emblazoned with the bar's logo hurried to August's side. He took the microphone from her outstretched hand, then offered her an elbow.

Samson frowned as unfamiliar jealousy stabbed at him. A flash of light caught his eye, and he realized August was holding a white cane. Had her eye condition progressed to the point where she now needed adaptive aids? How long had her vision been this way? He shook his head. Her lack of sight wasn't relevant, and she hadn't let it slow her down. She was still singing and had such an incredible voice. She crossed into the light, and damn if she didn't have the body to go with the voice.

But that voice. Samson and August had come a long way from high school musicals and choirs. He had been in the band, and she was always on the stage. And here she was, still dazzling audiences with her beautiful voice.

"You were amazing!" Samson praised. He watched her closely for any signs of recognition. She furrowed her brow, but that was about it. Disappointment deflated his enthusiasm. Maybe she didn't remember him after all.

⌒

August River nodded as she extended the collapsible cane. Several other people crowded her as she carefully made her way away from the stage. Though this was her first time at the Council for the Blind's monthly social event, being around this group of strangers gave her a sense of comfort. She didn't have to explain her vision. If she bumped into someone or something, the fumble was dismissed instead of met with derision. Being surrounded by blind or visually impaired people filled her with a sense of belonging.

Of course, there was a similar organization back home. But it was nothing like this group. August was here tonight because of Father Time, an older man who had been hired by her younger son to find out who had murdered her ex-husband.

She bit the inside of her cheek. She wouldn't have spent her money on finding out who killed the whoring bastard, but she understood that her son needed some sense of closure. Father Time's detective agency had provided that. Not only had he discovered who had murdered Dicky Williams, but his wife, and the owner of a catering company.

Now, people surrounded August to congratulate her on a job well done. Singing was her passion. She could lose herself in the music and bring her audience along for the emotional ride.

Hesitating, she sensed the area around her. She could hear laughter, conversation, and music playing at a volume that added ambiance and did not overwhelm the senses. The rich aroma of tomato sauce and melted cheese drifted through the cool air. Something pleasant like the forest after a spring rain tickled her nostrils. The scent niggled a memory, and she inhaled appreciatively.

"Like I said, you have an amazing voice."

August tilted her head toward the speaker. There was something familiar about the sexy voice. "You're still here?" she demanded. Something about the man's voice and nearness ignited long-dormant desires, and she didn't like it.

"I'm here all night." He moved closer, his arm brushing against hers.

She heard the smile through his words. "You make a habit of trying out lame lines on unsuspecting women?"

He chuckled. The deep throaty sound sent a shiver of awareness through her bloodstream. *What the blenders is this?* She was too old to get distracted by a smooth-talking man. She had enough of those to last a lifetime.

"I like your style," Samson said.

"You don't even know me," she scoffed.

There was that laugh again. Slow, sensual, and teasing. She knew that laugh. Knew the voice. No, it couldn't be. She stepped back, but the man followed. The way he stood in her personal bubble spoke of familiarity. His clean, crisp scent and the slow slide of his fingers on her forearm brought back memories long forgotten. Memories of a stolen kiss between classes. Sharing an ice cream cone beneath the bleachers. The first time she gave herself to him. She slammed the lid on that memory and stepped away from his gentle caress.

"Samson?" she whispered, unable to speak any louder.

"And here I thought you'd totally forgotten me."

She closed her eyes as his warm breath tickled her ear. She had never forgotten her first. Samson was a lot of firsts for her. The most significant being the first boy she ever had sex with. Desire and need sizzled through her system. Could what they did so long ago be called sex? She didn't think so. They'd been stupid kids, and she'd pledged her heart to him. What had she known about love at 16?

"I never forgot you."

He pressed closer, his body warm, hard, and strong against her softer one. "Do you remember the first time I saw you? You were singing then too."

August tightened her hold on the handle of her cane as the memory washed over her. That had been sixth, no seventh-grade drama class. He'd waited for her then too.

He would not do this to her. Not here. Not now. Too much time had passed, and too many pieces of her heart were missing. "Go away, Samson. You don't know me anymore."

"So give me a chance to know you."

August bit her lip. There were so many reasons for her to walk away and not take a chance. "I don't think that's a good idea." As she turned to leave, he caught her hand. A current ran up her arm and swept along her nipples. She tugged on her hand, and he released her.

"I'm sorry. You just seem like you need someone."

"Are you trying to say I'm helpless?" she demanded coolly. "The only thing I don't do anymore is drive. I am more than capable of taking care of myself, and somehow I've even managed to raise children. And…."

"Whoa. Whoa. Pump your brakes. So not what I meant," Samson sputtered. "I didn't mean to insult you. I just meant you look sad, and I hate to see a beautiful, talented woman such as yourself look so sad." He lowered his voice. "Especially when I know you always had an easy smile. Right, Sol?"

"You always thought my smile was like the sun," she muttered as she thought of the nickname.

"You remembered."

The sincerity and pleasure in his voice stalled any further tirade and chipped at the wall around her heart. "Yeah" was all she managed to say.

An enthusiastic man belted out an off-key rendition of Barry White's "First, Last, Everything." What he lacked in vocals, he made up for in energy. The crowd sang with him.

"You must get that a lot? People assuming you can't take care of yourself," Samson clarified.

Despite her resolve to remain aloof, she said, "yes."

"Frankly, the biggest reason I volunteer with this organization is how all of you inspire me to be better. How you never let your sight stop you."

Truth rang in his words. "Thanks," she grudgingly said.

He laughed. "That hurt, didn't it?"

"A little," she admitted with a short laugh.

"Much better," he praised. "Your eyes light up when you smile."

August ducked her head, her braids brushing her shoulders and cheeks. She didn't want to acknowledge the pleasure of his words. Or how his cologne was doing odd things to her. She fought the urge to lean in and deeply inhale the man's scent. He smelled so good, like sin and smoke. If this had been another time and place and her heart were not so damaged, she'd flirt a little. As it was, there were more important things in life than flirting with a man with a sense of humor. And she did love a sense of humor.

"Did I say something wrong? You're looking sad again?"

This man was way too observant. She had to get away before he saw something else in her eyes or face. Or she could just get better at not showing her emotions. "No. Are you here with anyone?" She hoped this question would deflect his attention from her back to his companion. For the blink of a heartbeat, she found herself envious of his faceless companion. Even when they were younger, he was popular with other girls. Why should now be any different?

"If that's a sly way of asking if I'm in a relationship, the answer is no."

He was single! Excitement leaped through her, and she ruthlessly squashed it. What was wrong with her? Wasn't one failed relationship enough? Did she need to add the distraction of finding someone else attractive? Then again, finding a man attractive wasn't a relationship. It was human. A perfectly feminine response to an eligible male, especially one she had history and chemistry with. One who still made her pulse dance.

Well, whatever it was, she needed to stop it. Hormones, lust, and the whole ball of sex complicated life. And she didn't need any more complications at this stage in her life. Wasn't raising a small child fulfilling enough? Especially when said child's parents had suffered horrible deaths? Yeah. She didn't need this smooth-talking, good-smelling man to cloud her rational judgment. Or did she? She shook her head. Wasn't there room in her heart for a good man?

"There's that look again," Samson said.

"You know if you went and talked to someone else, how I look wouldn't bother you," she snapped.

He laughed.

Was he laughing at her now? What was wrong with this guy? She wasn't being nice; truthfully, her actions were bordering on rudeness. Yet, he was laughing like she'd told a joke.

⌒

Samson allowed his gaze to rove over the curvy woman with long sisterlocks. The form-fitting leggings and hip-skimming tunic showed off lush sexiness. When he finally focused on her face, her full lips pouted in a slight frown. He wanted to see her eyes light with laughter as they had before. As they had when they were teens, not dim with sadness.

"You made a beeline all the way over here just to tell me I can sing?" she queried. "You do realize I'm blind. Surely, there must be others here for you to interact and laugh at besides me."

An easy chuckle left his lips. "Of course. You must have some vision if you saw me make a beeline over here," he countered.

She rolled those beautiful brown eyes.

What happened in her life to bring such sadness to her eyes? She used to be so open and carefree. Now it was a challenge to maintain a simple conversation with her. "I haven't heard a voice like yours in a long time. You could give Jill Scott a run for her money."

"Huh," was all she said.

Okay, not the reaction he expected. "So, do you always react this way when someone gives you a compliment?"

She shrugged, a careless lift of one shoulder. "I suppose the appropriate answer would be thank you, but I know I can sing, and Jill Scott is one of my favorite artists." She turned slightly. "Besides, the energy of the crowd is all the thanks I need. I'm surprised you don't remember that about me, Samson."

He caught the whisper of sarcasm in her last sentence. He had to bite back a grin. He remembered how self-assured she was about her talent and didn't need praise. It was good to see she still had some sass. He liked that. "You and my mother are the only ones who call me by my given name. Around here, I go by Stx."

"Sticks?" She repeated. "Like the things that come off trees?"

Now he laughed. "No. Like the River Styx in Greek mythology only without the y."

"How did you get saddled with a moniker like that?"

He pulled a pair of drumsticks from his back pocket and tapped a quick rhythm on a nearby column. "I'm the drummer for a band. We could definitely use someone with your voice."

"You always did like banging on things," she quipped.

"I did enjoy banging you," he said in a seductive purr.

Her eyes widened at the double entendre. "Those days are long gone."

He captured her hand and placed a kiss on the middle of her palm. From the close distance, he noted the dilation of her pupils and the slight inhale of breath at his actions. "It seems a bit of the old spark is still there."

She swallowed several times before she found her voice. "Go away, Samson," she leaned on his name.

He grinned. "I'm still going to call you Sol, even though your sunny disposition is in question."

A smile teased the corners of her mouth. "At least you're original."

"I try."

"Thanks for the trip down memory lane." August shifted. "Well, I'm going to mingle since it is my first time here."

Unable to resist, he matched her steps. "I could introduce you to some of the group. They really are a great bunch of people."

"If you're not blind or visually impaired, are you here with a spouse or significant other?"

"Is that the only reason I would be here? I could be here to support the cause."

"That or pick up women," she quipped.

He laughed. "You still speak your mind."

"Pretty much," she agreed.

"The really cool thing about the Council for the Blind is they allow membership to anyone interested in furthering their agenda. Quite frankly, I enjoy getting involved in their events. Aside from the monthly socials, they sponsor several public events throughout the year. They also bring awareness to those with blindness. Did you know they even offer scholarships to visually impaired students? There's job training seminars and monthly meetings where they invite all sorts of speakers. One month, they had a man who makes clocks."

"What's so great about a man who makes clocks? I make bread."

"He's totally blind," he answered. Samson placed a hand at the small of August's back and guided her to where a couple, a man with an apron and a petite brunette, stood.

"Hello, Geneva. Kyle," Samson greeted. "I have Sol with me. She gave us that lovely rendition of A Long Walk."

"Hey, Stx. Great to meet you, Sol. You have a great voice!" Geneva praised, a slight lisp on her words. "Is this your first time here?"

"Yes," August answered. "Mr. Time invited me."

Clicking filled the silence, and a tall, lanky man with an afro joined them. "This is my husband, Jethro. Jethro, this is Sol, and it's her first time here."

"Great to meet you, Sol," Jethro said. "You came on a perfect day. Abigail and Time are getting married." He placed an arm around his wife's shoulders. "Have you met any of the others yet?"

"I'm taking her around now," Samson said. "I'll try not to overwhelm her with too many people."

"It was great meeting you, Sol. Hopefully, you'll join us for more activities. Tomorrow afternoon we have a self-defense class."

"Really?" Interest lit Sol's voice.

"It's very empowering," Geneva answered. "Joshua and Amelia are really good at teaching us what we need to know."

"Wow. I'm so glad I came tonight."

Sincerity rang in August's words, and Samson gave a bittersweet smile as he saw some of the sadness recede from

August's face. Why hadn't she greeted him with the same enthusiasm? Why couldn't he have the same response?

Samson and August had been near inseparable as teens until she went off to school and he to the... He glanced at Sol. Could he have been holding a torch for her all this time? Was that why he was so enamored with her now? Or was it a form of familiarity? He shook his head. No. He'd never gotten over her. Never forgot about her in the interim years. Seeing her again provoked a streak of protectiveness in him he hadn't felt in a long time. And why was it so important for him to see her smile? Why did he care that sadness clung to her like wet cotton? Maybe because someone who sang with such passion didn't seem like she should be sad.

"You know, I can mingle on my own," August said once they'd moved away from Geneva and Jethro.

"I know you're very capable of mingling. This just makes it easier."

"Do you act as escort for all the new people who arrive?" she quipped.

"No, just the ones I have history with."

Stifling a laugh, August shook her head.

"You truly have a beautiful smile," he stated. "You should do it more often."

She ducked her head, hiding her expression from him. "You know, there's just not enough to smile about these days," she murmured.

"Yo! Stx!" A deep voice called over the din of noise.

Samson glanced over his shoulder, giving the speaker a nod of acknowledgment. "That's my cue. We need to get on stage." He touched her hair before sliding a braid behind her ear. "Save me a seat. I want to make sure you wear a smile when you go home tonight." Samson had to resist the urge to lean in and kiss those pouting, full lips. Even the way he brushed her hair was natural. Kissing her would be the same way. He loved women but never reacted as strongly as he did to August. He allowed his gaze to linger on and over her.

She had soft, lush womanly curves of bygone pinup girls. Now that she was all woman, would she still be as passionate and adventurous as she'd been in their teens?

"You're staring," she said.

"I like what I see. He stepped close to take in the faint scent of lavender clinging to her skin. "I've always liked what I've seen. Save me a seat. Please?"

A smile twitched at her lips. "Only because you asked so nicely."

He chuckled and muttered, "You do something to me." Before he realized what he was doing, he dropped his mouth to hers.

She stiffened in his arms before she placed her palms against his chest. Was she going to shove him away or pull him closer? He snaked an arm around her hips and feathered his lips over hers. Time stood still as the past collided with the present. They were two teenagers again with their entire lives before them. She was willing and pliant, and her mouth was lush and sweet. He could lose himself in just kissing her.

Hoots and catcalls invaded the tender moment. Samson stepped back, and August swayed against him. "We've got to do that again!" He kissed her again and left. He glanced behind him. She was still a little dazed. A wide grin split his face as he rushed onstage and behind the drum set. Before he sat, he adjusted his erection to a more comfortable position.

"New girlfriend?" Marcus Andrews inquired as he draped the strap of his guitar over his shoulder.

Samson twirled one of the wooden drumsticks between his fingers. "Nope. She's the woman I'm gonna marry."

Chapter Two

August had no idea what had just happened. Had he really kissed her? And why didn't she shove him away? For a moment, her brain and body were transported to simpler times when love for this boy was all-consuming. But he was no longer a boy.

She had a vague recollection of placing her hands on his chest to do that, but somehow between the soft cotton of his shirt and the hard defined pecs beneath the material, she'd been stuck. Samson had grown into a sexy piece of man. A man who seemed to have grown more potent with maturity. Like liquor, he got better with age.

He'd always been a good kisser. She sighed. Not to mention how cool, firm, and commanding his lips moved on hers.

The kiss was so unexpected. She could still feel his lips pressed to hers. And her panties were damp as well. Wanton lust simmered in her veins. She had no intention of rekindling old flames or finding a bed buddy or intimacy at this social. She came to socialize, become active in the blind community, and make friends.

But Samson could be my special friend. She shook her head, trying to dislodge the thought. August didn't need any special friends. Especially not ones who could kiss her into an orgasm. Was she so sex-starved that one kiss was enough to melt her panties and send her libido into over-drive? And she promised to save him a seat. She could not sit next to him and not think about his lips. Or how his grown man's body would feel against hers. Was he still tick-lish? Did he still like making love in the shower or holding hands after lovemaking?

She sniffed the air. A bit of his scent clung to her clothes. How was she supposed to get through the rest of the night with his scent on her clothes? Every time she inhaled, her nipples tightened.

"How do you know Stx?" a simpering honeyed voice demanded. "You know he doesn't go around kissing random women."

"That's good to know. If he did, I'm sure he'd be on a list somewhere." August didn't like the woman's tone.

The woman introduced herself in the same simpering tone. "I haven't seen you at one of these before. I'm Emerald."

"How do you know Stx?"

"Oh, we're partners," Emerald stated glibly. "I always have his back."

Was that a note of jealousy August heard in the other woman's voice? August nearly laughed. "What do you do to have his back?" she queried. "I'm sure Stx is very glad he has you on his side."

"We're cops in the bomb squad." Pride clung to Emerald's voice. "We're part of an exclusive group."

"Sounds interesting." August shifted away. "Thanks for sharing." August walked away, moving her cane from side to side before the other woman could say anything else. *Samson is in the bomb squad?* That was enough reason for her not to get involved with him. He could leave one day and not come home. She'd had enough of men leaving her and not coming back.

Her cane hit something metallic, and she stopped.

"It's just a chair," a friendly voice called. "Have a seat and listen to the music."

Grateful for the interruption of her wayward thoughts, August found the back of the chair and pulled it out enough for her to sit.

"You came on a good night," he continued. "Abigail and Time are getting married, there's karaoke, and Stx's band is playing. By the way, you were great up there."

"Thanks."

"Would you like me to grab you a plate or something to drink?"

Now that he mentioned it, she was thirsty. "Water would be great."

"I'm Avery. My wife Penelope and I own a bakery downtown."

"Are you blind too?"

Avery chuckled. "No, but she is. You should see some of the cakes and candies she makes."

August replayed the words in her head. It wasn't so much what he said but how he said it. The love and admiration in his voice made August momentarily envious that she had no one who felt that way about her. Samson had been willing long ago before life stepped in and spit all over her.

"I'll be right back with your water." A chair scraped, and footsteps echoed away.

August sat back, grateful for the respite. Sticks tapped before a male voice counted down, "3... 2... 1." She tapped her foot in time with an uptempo beat and a complex guitar solo.

Vibrations flowed through her chair, and a slight breeze touched her face.

"I set the bottle next to your left hand, and there's a cup of ice next to it," Avery explained. "Let me know if you'd like anything else."

"Thanks." She was a little surprised she could still talk without yelling over the music.

"I saw Emerald talking to you. I hope she wasn't too rude."

"I think she was staking her claim," August said dismissively.

"Be careful around her. She didn't look too happy about the kiss you and Stx shared," he warned.

It took every bit of willpower for August not to flinch from embarrassment. "Did everybody see that exchange?" She would never live this down.

Avery chuckled. "A few."

Rhythmic swishing and tapping moved closer. "I'm back!" a female voice announced.

"Sol, this is my wife, Penelope," Avery said.

"Good to meet you, Penelope," August greeted. "You own a bakery?"

Penelope let out an infectious giggle that made August smile. August didn't know much about this couple, but she got the impression they were good people.

"We do. It's been in my family for a few generations now. You were incredible up there. Have you thought about singing professionally?"

August thought of the singing group she'd been a part of in her early teens. They'd gone to New York and sang for producers of a well-known record label. The execs only wanted her talent and not the group. She hadn't been willing to leave her friends behind. How different would her life have been if she'd said yes?

"It's a hard way to make a living," August stated.

"It certainly sounded like you were having a great time up there." Penelope's easy manner put August at ease.

"I love singing. I made a promise to myself that I would do more," August began. "Life is so short. It doesn't pay to be afraid all the time."

"No, it doesn't," Penelope agreed.

The conversation hit a lull, and August tuned into the music. Her foot still tapped to the beat. She had a hard time sitting still.

"The band is really good," August said.

"They're a favorite part of our karaoke nights. Abigail's has an open mic night a couple times a month. They're usually here," Penelope explained.

"Most of the band members are off-duty police officers," Avery said.

"Really?" August perked up. So Emerald hadn't been lying. Although August couldn't fathom why the woman would lie.

"You should ask him about it. He does some really cool things."

"Will do," August promised.

The music shifted to something slower. The band was now doing a cover of "Part-time Lover." The lead singer was decent, and he made up for what he lacked in vocals with enthusiasm.

August listened to the steady beat interpreted with fills and an impromptu drum solo. Samson was good. Really good. Even better than he'd been in high school. She wondered if he could keep beat like that in bed?

Her lust simmered. Where had that thought come from? The last thing she needed was to fantasize about a man who only knew her as a teenage love. A man who had kissed her as if she belonged to him. A man who ignited a long-dormant passion. She stood abruptly. "I think I'm gonna find the dance floor." She extended her cane and moved before anyone could stop her.

She maneuvered over smooth wood until the ball tip of her cane flashed over something metallic. The edge of the dance floor, perhaps? Tile echoed beneath her shoes as she took her next three steps. She smiled when she reached the dance floor. She folded her cane, placed it beneath her arm, and moved to the beat of the music.

Stx almost dropped his sticks when he caught sight of August swaying on the dance floor. For a moment, he was mesmerized by her gyrating hips. The woman had moves. Would she be as good or better in bed? The thought sent a spasm of lust through his veins. His foot stutter-stepped on the foot pedal.

He quickly recovered but not before the lead singer sent him a quizzical glance. Stx saluted him with a drumstick and kept playing. Sweat trickled between Stx's shoulder blades and down his spine. He had to concentrate on the music if he was going to keep beat. Yet he couldn't stop his gaze from straying to the woman dropping it like it was hot on the dance floor. The stick slipped from his left hand, flipped through the air, spun as it careened off the silver trim of the high hat, and rolled out of sight. Without missing a beat, Stx played with one stick until he grabbed another from the holder fastened to the side of the tom-toms.

Marcus swiveled to look, and Stx grinned. Marcus shook his head as he strummed, the song almost over. When it ended, Stx wiped the sweat from his face with the back of his hand. Applause swelled as the last note reverberated off the rafters.

"Give us a few, and we'll be back to entertain you again," Johnny promised. He turned off the mic before facing Stx. "What was that?"

Stx looked past Johnny to the woman now surrounded by a muscular man with shoulder-length sandy hair. The man's arm draped around the waist of a mocha-skinned woman with vibrant red hair. Next to them was a taller black man with silver hair and a matching beard and mustache. The silver-haired man was linking arms with a peachy-skinned strawberry blonde. All of them were smiling.

Why hadn't Sol smiled at him like that? He felt a tiny shard of jealousy. Sol seemed so relaxed and happy with the two couples, yet she'd been cool and distant with him—until he kissed her.

Kissing her had been the best decision of his life. Beneath that cool exterior lurked the fire he vividly remembered. And he wasn't imagining things. It was as if they had never been apart. He wanted to pursue how hot he could make her burn. But could he get past the sadness shadowing her eyes?

Johnny turned to follow his gaze. "Ah. The siren with the voice. You know she could replace Mira," he mused. "She has the voice and the stage presence." He swung his gaze back to Stx. "Then again, she may be too much of a distraction for you."

Stx grinned. "If she's on stage, I won't be distracted."

Johnny bent, then came up with the errant drumstick. "I'll believe that when I see it."

Stx accepted the stick, placing it in the holder on the side of the toms. "If you don't mind, I'm gonna go keep my future smiling." He tucked his sticks in his back pocket, leaving the stage with his eyes focused on Sol.

August smelled Samson's crisp, masculine scent before he even spoke.

"You've got some amazing moves," Samson murmured close to her ear. "How about we dance to the next song?"

His warm breath against her ear sent shivers straight to her nipples. What was this man doing to her, and why did she keep reacting like this? After the kiss, the last place she needed to be was in his arms. August shook her head. "I'm good. You shoulda told me you were a cop." She heard how clipped her voice sounded.

"You don't like men in uniform?" he teased.

She loved men in uniform and especially loved that Samson was still a drummer in a band. But she couldn't tell him that. "Your partner has a thing for you. She warned me off."

"Who?" Puzzlement clouded his voice.

"Emerald, I think her name was."

He chuckled. "Yeah, she is a little protective. I've had a few bad relationships." He ushered August toward the food-laden table. "I'll talk to her about it."

"Bad relationships?"

"Yeah. When you're in my line of work, hours aren't conducive to relationships. The last few relationships fizzled and burned. They couldn't handle me being on call or out of touch. Or the uncertainty that I could be injured, maimed, or killed on the job."

"Those things could happen to anyone getting out of the bathtub," she scoffed.

He laughed. "I like the way you think. Are you hungry? I'm starving, and Abigail always has a nice spread."

August realized she was starving as silverware rattled against plates, and the scent of fried chicken, spicy meatballs, and melted cheese wafted through the air. Plus, the cardio on the dance floor stimulated her appetite. "I am. What they got?"

"Looks like a variety of sliders, burgers, turkey, ham. Fried Chicken, uh—" his voice moved away, "a couple of different salads. I think one is broccoli. The other is green salad with tomatoes, cucumbers, and some sort of cheese. Oh sweet! Someone brought shrimp cocktail. There are mini meatball subs and one of those trays with the veggies and cheeses on it."

"I'll take one of the turkey sliders and a bit of the broccoli salad," she said.

"Anything else?" He placed the requested items on her plate, then turned to heap food on his own. "You sure you don't want any veggies? Or cheese?"

August bit her lip. "Just one carrot."

He placed the carrot and a dollop of the dip on her plate. "You don't eat much anymore, do you?" He led her to a two-top.

"This isn't where we were sitting earlier," she protested.

"It's a little quieter, and we can get to know each other. Be back with our drinks."

His footsteps faded. August checked the time on her watch and saw there was about an hour left of the social. She scanned the room, wondering where the time had gone. Flashes of light, shapes, and shadows flickered. Noise and laughter filled the air, but her senses weren't overwhelmed. Was this a typical social night for Abigail's Place? And how did she end up with the drummer from the band as her escort? Weren't there other women he could focus his interest on?

The fact he settled his attention on her sent a warm rush of pleasure through her body. It had been a few months since a man had paid her any attention. She was not looking for a man, especially not when she had a six-year-old to raise. Maybe she would tell Samson about her little guy and see what he said about his interest in her then.

A lull in the voices and music drew her attention to the scrape of shoes on the hardwood. She turned her head in that direction.

"I got us a couple of waters." Plastic crinkled a moment before something heavy clunked on the table. "And glasses with lemon and ice."

"Thanks," August murmured.

The chair legs scraped along the floor, and the table moved as Samson settled into place. August placed her hands on the table to steady it.

"Sorry about that," he mumbled.

"Before this goes any further, you need to know that I'm raising a six-year-old and take my mom responsibilities very seriously."

Chapter Three

Stx grinned. The expression on Sol's face was so serious. Did she truly expect him to dismiss her because she had a kid? He nearly laughed out loud. He popped a meatball from the sub in his mouth, chewing to give himself time to compose the appropriate answer. While he formulated the answer, he studied her face. Whether she knew it or not, she had a very expressive face. Her eyes told the story. If anyone chose to look, everything Sol felt was in her eyes. Even if her full mouth wasn't smiling, her eyes were.

"I love kids," he finally said, working hard not to laugh when Sol's lips formed a perfect "O." "I know I'm a bit old to start a family." He chewed again. "Which is another reason my previous relationships failed. I wanted kids, but they didn't."

"I thought that would be a turnoff. For most guys, it is."

He reached across the table and covered her hand. When she tried to pull away, he retained his hold. "I'm not most guys. I know what I want, and I'm not afraid to pursue you again."

Sol shook her head. "I'm still recovering from a divorce. You might want to look elsewhere." She pushed the food around on her plate. "I'm not the same girl from high school."

"How long were you married?" he asked quietly.

"Nearly twenty-two years." Pain skittered through her irises.

"What happened?"

"Bottom line? He wanted a younger woman. She needed him more than I did." Sol popped a cube of cheese in her mouth, chewed, then swallowed. "Well, that's enough of that. I really can't say my piece to either of them because they're both dead now."

Stx sat back, stunned by her candor. "That has to be a heavy burden. Both of them dead, and you're raising their kid, I presume?"

"Actually, just hers. She got pregnant by someone else and was going to abort the baby. And I, like a fool, opened my mouth and said I'd raise the baby."

Intrigued, Stx set down his fork and leaned forward. "You can't make a statement like that and not give all the details. You willingly raised another woman's child, and somehow she ended up married to your ex?"

Sol nodded, a wry smile twisting her luscious lips. "And then they both end up dead." She finally popped the broccoli floret in her mouth. "Let's talk about something else."

"How about you give me your number, and we can set up a real date," he suggested.

"Why?" she said with suspicion.

"Because you're worth the time. You were always worth my time."

Before she could respond, vibrations and chimes filled the air. The same alert surrounded the entire building.

"What's going on?" Sol asked.

"I'm on call this weekend, and we may have to go," Stx explained, not bothering to mask his disappointment. He wanted to spend a little more time with this woman. He had to know what prompted her to care for someone else's child.

"All right." After a moment's hesitation, Sol rattled off ten numbers.

Stx hastily typed the digits into his phone and then composed a text. "I sent you a text with my name and number. Read it later," he told her. He stood and swept his fingers gently down her cheek. "I will let you know I made it home in one piece."

When August's son came to pick her up an hour later, she felt more at ease. She felt like she'd finally found a home or a space where she belonged. She would definitely become a member of the Council and get more involved in their activities.

"How was it?" DJ asked, offering his arm to his mother.

"It was a lot of fun. Abigail and Time got married." She grasped DJ's elbow, allowing him to lead her from the bar. "There was a live band and karaoke."

"Did you wow them with your vocals?"

August laughed. "I just sing. Got a lot of compliments, and the drummer from the band wants me to try out for their band. He also happens to be a friend from high school."

"Sounds like fun. Was he a good friend in high school, or did he break your heart?" DJ teased.

"We drifted apart." She shrugged. "Then I met your dad, and the rest is history."

"Maybe I should meet this friend of yours."

Cool air swirled and chilled her heated skin. She shivered in the breeze. "It got colder."

"Yeah. I got the heat on in the car."

Sol settled into the front seat.

A little voice piped up from the backseat. "Hi, Mom!"

August turned in her seat, smiling. "Hi, Issac. Were you good for your brother?"

"Mm-hmm," the child answered. DJ bought me a Kinder egg. I got a dinosaur."

"Cool. Let's see." She held out her hand for the toy. Isaac placed a small piece of plastic in her palm.

"Its arms and head move."

"Roar!" August mimicked a dino.

Isaac laughed. "Did you have fun? Can I go with you next time?"

"We'll see," she said, turning to face front. "I have definitely found a place where I belong."

"That's good, Mom." DJ slipped the car into gear. "It's good to make new friends."

August brushed her fingertips over her lips, thinking of the kiss once more. "Yeah. New friends."

⌒

Three days later, August stood on one side of a plastic waist-high gate. Three dogs of varying sizes and colors raced from one end of the room to the other. Happy woofs and yaps reverberated off the ceiling. Beside her, a harnessed yellow lab whined softly.

"Quiet," August admonished. "I'll let you join your little friends in a minute. She unhooked the side, slipped in, then locked the gate again. With practiced ease, she unhooked the harness, looped it over her shoulder, and tightened her hold on the leash.

"Sit," she ordered. The dog sat. "Stay." She placed her free hand on the clip attached to his collar. The dog trembled but did not move. "Good boy," she praised. She released him. "Now, take a break!"

He was off, a streak of yellow fur as he raced back and forth with the other dogs. Using the wall as a guide, Sol walked to where she kept the water bowls. Of the four bowls that were out, only two were empty. She filled the empty bowls from the nearby sink before topping off the other two bowls. No sooner had she set them down than she heard noisy slurping. Again, the dogs took off running. August stayed on the outside of the square-shaped play area that was a bit smaller than a school gymnasium.

"How long have you been doing this?" a reedy male voice asked.

"Doing what?" August queried.

"Training dogs."

"Couple of years. I mostly train simple things."

"So you didn't train your guide dog?"

"No, but he helps with some of the other dogs when I need him to," August answered. She pulled four bags of treats from the cupboard over the sink.

"If you had to, could you train a guide dog?"

August paused. "I could, but training a dog for that particular skill would require a lot of time. It isn't the same as getting a dog just to sit, stay or lay down," she explained. She closed the cupboard door. "I'm sorry, your name again?"

"David, I'm surprised after all this time you still don't remember my voice." His tone held a playful note.

"Sometimes it takes a bit to match voices." She nodded, carrying the treat bags back to the counter near the gate.

"Right. Misty is your dog. Have you had any other issues with her chewing on the lead?"

"The bitters you suggested did the trick. When I distract her with an actual chew toy, she leaves the lead alone." A smile filled his voice.

"And recalling her?"

For the last few weeks, August had assisted David and Misty with getting his dog's attention.

"Much better. When I release Misty in the yard, she comes back almost as soon as I call her name. Especially when she thinks I have a treat in hand."

"Do you keep a treat in hand?"

David chuckled. "I switch it up between praise and treats. Can't have my girl gaining too much weight." H--e laughed.

August smiled. "Indeed. Did you have any other questions?"

"Now that you mention it, are you free Saturday night?"

"I'm afraid I don't have any classes on Saturday evening."

David coughed. "Not for the dog. To have dinner with me."

"Oh." She couldn't think of anything else to say.

David finally broke the awkward silence. "I'm sorry. I did kinda spring that on you. Forget I asked. I'm just killing time until Misty is done next door."

August nodded. A grooming and pet supply store occupied the space next door. Many clients found her via that business, so she referred all of her clients to the groomer.

"You did surprise me, and it's very sweet of you to ask," she began gently.

"But you're already taken," he finished.

Was that disappointment she heard, or was there an edge of something else in his tone?

"Sort of. Someone else asked for my Saturday night. I'm sorry."

He drummed his fingers on the counter. "It was a long shot anyway. A beautiful woman like you always has suitors." A chime trilled. "One moment while I answer this."

August shook her head. How hadn't she realized David was interested in her? She thought over their last several encounters. He was always helpful. He often stayed to clean after classes or came early to help set up. And often, like now, while his dog was being groomed, he hung out with August. She hadn't noticed the obvious signs. Maybe it was because she hadn't been interested in pursuing anyone. She still wasn't sure if she wanted to go on her date Saturday, but she hadn't been able to say no to Samson.

The spark she and Samson shared long ago was a banked fire waiting to be stoked into roaring life. A part of her wanted their love again. A wet nose brushed her hand. She glanced down to find her guide, Riley, nudging her fingers. She gave him a quick scratch behind the ears before he ran off again. She smiled. No matter how hard he played with the other dogs, he always checked in to make sure she was okay.

"Could I give you a hand?" David moved next to her, the sleeve of his shirt brushing her bare arm.

Bells chimed and clapped against the heavy glass door as it opened. "I've got a delivery," a hoarse voice called.

"How about I get the door for you?" he suggested.

"That would be great." The wind lifted her hair as David breezed by. Two of the dogs nudged her knees. She stroked each head as it grazed her fingertips. "You guys must know

I've got treats for you." She emitted a soft whistle, and the four dogs lined up. "Good boys and girl," she praised. She clicked the lead to her guide's collar and settled him in heel position —to her left side as she touched the other dogs. They all stayed put except for the occasional thump or swish of a tail against the floor. "Down!"

She listened carefully as soft sliding signaled the animals were now on their bellies. Tails thumped the floor.

"Stay."

She backed away slowly, and not one animal moved. "Good job," she praised with enthusiasm. She went down the line and gave each dog a treat.

The bells chimed again. A faint thud met August's ears, and she re-harnessed her guide. "Thanks, Dave," she called. She clicked her tongue, leading the way back to another dog run.

"No problem. I set your package on the counter. Misty is ready, so I'll see you at the next class."

"Good deal."

"Looks like the groomer is getting a delivery too."

"Flip the sign for me on your way out," August called.

"Will do." A flutter and jingle signaled David's departure.

Once the dogs had been relieved and the three hanging out in their crates, Sol walked to the front counter, intent on opening the package. It was probably more treats or dog food, but the package hadn't sounded heavy when David placed it on the counter. Maybe paper supplies?

She reached for a box cutter and stopped. Tilting her head to one side, she listened. Something was ticking. Faint. She dismissed it as the clock on the wall. She could usually hear the timepiece when it was quiet. Yet...she stepped closer to the counter. The ticking echoed. Setting the box cutter on top of the package, she pulled the cardboard closer. She had just sliced the tape when something heavy hit the door, and the chimes jangled in alarm.

"Stop!"

August froze, the blade still stuck in the tape. "Who is that?" She couldn't keep the annoyance from her voice.

"August. Stop what you're doing and step away from the box."

The urgency in Dave's voice sent a swell of alarm through her. "What's wrong?"

Footsteps hurried nearer. "We think there's a bomb inside."

Chapter Four

Adrenaline rushed through Stx's system. He carefully rehearsed the steps he would take once he was at the potential bomb site. He considered that the call could be a false alarm. *Who sent ticking bombs through the mail?* The days of the Unabomber were long over. Homemade devices were more likely to appear at well-populated events rather than, he doubled-checked his screen, a dog groomer.

"You think someone was disgruntled about Fido's haircut?" Emerald scoffed. "This has got to be some sort of joke."

"Joke or not, we have to check it out."

She flicked a glance at him through the rearview mirror. "So you ever make contact with that woman you met at the social?"

Stx heard the slight bite in Emerald's otherwise casual tone.

"Haven't had a chance other than a few texts. You could say we're getting reacquainted with one another. We knew each other as teens."

He didn't know why he felt compelled to tell Emerald he had a history with Sol, but his instincts warned him it was necessary. Somehow, he had to give Emerald the impression Sol would be one of the most important people in his life without alienating Emerald.

"She told me what you said to her at the social," he began quietly.

Now she glanced at him sharply. "I was only looking out for your best interests. Whenever you have a bad break-up, your head gets clouded. And that's not good when we work with things that go boom."

"I always check my emotions at the door," he stated, a bit defensively.

Emerald huffed. "We're headed to a scene, and you choose now to jump down my throat about some chick you wanna bang?" she demanded. "You were all over her until we got called away."

"The issue isn't my timing of this conversation. The issue is you're going behind my back to warn women away," he argued.

They paused to maneuver around vehicles at a red light.

Emerald shook her head. "This is so stupid."

"We spend a lot of hours together, Em. We have a good relationship, and I trust you to watch my back."

"But…" she prompted.

"But Sol is special, and she's going to be a huge part of my life when I'm not working." Stx studied his partner closely for any reaction. What he saw was a faint muscle tick in her jaw. If he hadn't been watching so close, he'd have missed the flicker of emotion, something akin to grief.

"Fair enough."

They fell silent. Even though some tension remained, Stx was grateful for the silence. For the first time, Stx noticed something that others had hinted. Was Emerald interested in him as a romantic partner and not just her work partner? He'd viewed Emerald as his friend, colleague, and work partner. Nothing more.

He stole a glance from the corner of his eye. Emerald was attractive if one liked the lean, athletic type.

He preferred a little more softness. Toned, but with womanly curves. Like Sol.

Every day he thanked God for being a part of the Council for the Blind. If he hadn't, he wouldn't have run into Sol again.

If he were honest with himself, he hadn't been looking for anyone, focusing on his career and getting his life together. But seeing and hearing Sol threw all that out the window. He'd lost his chance some twenty years ago. He wasn't going to let this opportunity pass him by. And this new chance meant prioritizing communication.

He and Sol had done more than exchange texts. They'd also spoken on the phone and planned a date for the coming weekend—his first day off in almost two months. He loathed that he hadn't been able to see her before this weekend, but such was the job. With winter looming, they needed to keep things moving. He was thankful football season was nearly over and that the big game between Michigan and Michigan State was being held in East Lansing. He wouldn't have to worry about over 100,000 people packed into a city with a residency of a tenth of that. And he didn't need to be on call to patrol diehard tailgaters for Molotov cocktails or any other incendiary items.

Emerald nosed the van onto a two-lane road. In the distance, two patrol cars blocked the driveways of a long building. He squinted. No, it was two buildings. The one on the right had a sign with a poodle in a tub of bubbles.

The building on the left had a sign sporting a large dog paw print with the words Enrichment Center.

Emerald parked behind a third squad car, and Stx stepped out. The area was fairly deserted, and only faint barking met his ears. Only the buildings would be affected if there were an explosive device on the premises. There were many open fields.

"Two packages were delivered to the shops. The owners of both businesses are on site."

"Where are the potential devices?" Stx asked.

"They're inside. One in the office. The other in plain view on the counter. "Both owners reported hearing ticking."

Nodding, Stx accepted a small remote-control vehicle. He piloted the little robot through the front of the groomers, and he and Emerald watched the progress on the LED screen. Stx would've preferred to be inside, but the remote approach would keep him safe. He found the box. Indeed, there was a faint ticking. Before he could maneuver the bot in place, a muffled pop made him jump. The screen went white before it returned to—

"Is that confetti?" Emerald asked incredulously.

Stx shoved the remote control in her hands. "Let's take a look."

Cordite and burning paper filled his nostrils as he entered the groomers. A thin pall of white smoke clung to the air and grew thicker as Stx made his way to the back of the store.

He carefully approached the office just in case there was another explosion. He checked his protective gear, then stepped into the office. A cursory check showed there were no other explosives present. However, sparkly paper covered every surface.

"Let's see if we can get the other device before it blows," he said into his mic.

"Copy that."

"Are you sure it's safe?" August demanded. "They wouldn't even let me get the rest of my dogs out."

"Ma'am, I've told you. You cannot retrieve the animals until the space has been cleared."

"Then send one of the officers in to let them out!" she snapped. "They're in the back. Away from where you'll be working."

August was near tears. She was frustrated, mad, and scared. It was one thing to keep her out for her safety, but those three dogs didn't deserve to be harmed. Next to her, her guide paced and nudged her knee.

"Please," August pleaded.

"We've got a couple from the bomb squad here now. When it's safe, I'll let you back in to get the dogs."

"You don't have any pets, huh?"

"Ma'am, pets can be replaced. You can't."

"What kind of logic is that?" she argued. "Those dogs belong to someone and are quite irreplaceable to their owners."

Stx caught part of the argument as he strolled from one business to the other. The woman's voice was familiar, but he was more occupied with getting to the device before it exploded. If he could get the device intact, it would save his squad time reconstructing it later. He and Emerald entered the neighboring building. Muted barking greeted them.

"Holy shit!" Emerald swore. "There are still dogs in here. She vaulted the gate as Stx went to the counter.

He found the discarded box cutter and noticed that the packing tape had a neat slit. He inserted a small dental mirror into the slit. A taped wire clung to the far side of the box flap. Had the person continued cutting, the device would've exploded. The ticking grew louder. Checking to make sure there were no other triggers on the box, Stx cut away a section until he could see the wires. He stared at the canister attacked to the wires and a timer. Ten seconds registered on the digital display.

Footsteps hurried toward him. "I let the dogs out. There's a fenced yard back there."

Stx held up a hand as he yanked out a wire. The timer stopped at three seconds. He carefully removed the canisters and placed them in a lead-lined box. Beneath the timer and bags of confetti was a thick sheet of paper

"What is it?" Emerald crowded closer.

Stx unfolded the paper. He gasped as he read, "This is only the beginning."

Chapter Five

August paced back and forth, and her guide followed. David hadn't given her time to get the dogs out. And now the barking had her whirling.

"Find the fence!"

Her guide immediately steered her around several bystanders to the edge of the parking lot where the grass met the asphalt.

"Ma'am!" the reedy-voiced officer called.

August ignored the man. He'd have to tackle her to keep her from checking on the dogs. Even her guide quick-stepped as he realized his friends were nearby. They reached the fence, and August ran her fingers along the chain link until she came to the gate. She let herself in, closing the gate behind her. Once she was certain the lock was secure, she walked through the inner gate. The dogs surrounded her, sniffing and panting at her feet.

She ran a hand over each. "I'm so glad you're all right," she cooed. "I'll have to thank whoever let you out." Tears slipped down her cheeks, and she dabbed them away with her shoulder. "That stupid cop would've let you three get blown up."

Chain rattling drew her attention to the fence.

"Ma'am, I need you to get behind the perimeter."

"All clear," crackled over the radio.

"You heard the voice," she sniffed. "All clear."

"You're still not."

"I'll take care of her," a sensual male voice stated.

"She's super stubborn and doesn't listen."

"I'm aware."

August stood still. Was that who she thought it was. "Samson?"

The gate rattled. Before the second door opened, the three dogs at Sol's feet stood and growled.

"Easy," she warned.

"Was that for me or the dogs?" Stx asked.

"Both." She waved her hand and made a circle with her index finger. "Why are you here?"

The dogs sat but emitted hoarse growls.

"Are you going to let me get closer or keep your guard dogs?"

"Did you let my dogs out?"

"That was my partner, Emerald. I disarmed the bomb."

"That idiot cop wouldn't let me back in to let them out. He said they could be replaced." There was no disguising the disdain in her voice. She was plenty mad and not going to hold her tongue. "And when I asked if he could send someone to let them into the yard—"

"The dogs are safe. The inside of the building is safe." Stx assured her quietly. "But right now, I need to talk to you."

Silence stretched between them. The dogs, sensing her indecision, laid down but kept a watchful eye on Stx. Every time he shifted, one of the dogs bore a fang.

"You know," Stx began conversationally. "There are better ways to see me before our big date."

"What?"

"I didn't realize you were so eager to see me. You could've sent a text instead of questionable boxes."

Sol opened her mouth to snap a retort before registering his teasing tone. She fought back a smile. "What I find amazing is they actually have a helmet big enough for your ego."

"That's not the only thing on me that's big," he stated huskily.

August shifted as his statement conjured an image of skin-to-skin contact under sex-scented, tangled sheets. "You're—" her voice cracked. She cleared her throat and tried again. "You're too full of yourself."

"It helps with the charm."

She laughed, and the earlier tension slid from her body. Realization struck, and she sobered.

"Was it a real bomb?"

August swayed as it fully hit her as to how close to death she had come. Stx caught her before she could fall. He led her to a nearby bench.

"I'm okay," she muttered. The enormity of what could've happened left her trembling. She wrapped her arms around her middle in a vain attempt to stop shaking. If David hadn't come in when he did, would she be sitting here with her dogs? Or would she be some unidentifiable lump of skin, leaving her children orphaned? Her adult children might survive the loss, but poor Isaac. What would happen to him? Would either of his siblings step up to care for him, or would they be too grief-stricken?

"Stop what you're thinking right now!"

The order slashed through the what-ifs and what could've like a knife. August focused on the voice and caught a glimpse of milk chocolate skin and a scruffy jawline. She focused on his mouth and the lush, full lips she wanted to kiss.

"There was a bomb in my space," she said slowly.

"It has been disabled, and your space is clear of any hazards," he answered gently. He cupped Sol's cheek. "I promise you are safe."

August blinked back the hot sting of tears, but a few still spilled down her cheeks. "Why would someone send me a bomb? I train dogs."

Stx swiped the moisture away with his thumb. "I promise I will find out who did this."

August nodded. "Whatever I can do to help."

"Let's go speak to some detectives. They'll have some questions for you."

Stx ducked his head beneath the hot spray of water. Closing his eyes, he lifted his face and allowed the spray to wash away the grime and sweat of the day. He had struggled to leave Sol in his colleagues' hands when all he wanted to do was gather her close and whisk her away to some place safe. But he knew he would see her that evening.

He reached for the musk-scented body wash, squirted a liberal amount in his palms, lathered the suds in his hair, and worked his way down his body. His muscles flexed and stretched as soap slid down the valleys and planes of old scars and wounds that told the story of an active life. He squirted more soap into his hands, lathered his pubes, and sighed at the semi-erection he'd sported since seeing Sol. No matter how many showers or other mind games he played to douse his libido, he stayed aroused.

After rinsing, Stx stepped out of the shower, reached for a towel, and dried off. A few minutes later, he was dressed. He stowed his dirty clothes in the overstuffed duffle, slung it over his shoulder, locked his locker, and left the locker room.

Tube lights glared off the industrial tile floor and beige walls. He took the steps two at a time and waved to one of the desk sergeants before striding into the night.

He paused at the sound of hurried footsteps. Emerald was making her way toward him, head down.

"I thought you'd never come out," she said once she was in speaking range.

"What's up?" He dug out his keys.

"Thought maybe you wanted to catch a bite to eat?" A hopeful note clung to her voice.

"Raincheck?" He walked toward his truck. "I've got plans."

"Oh."

Was that disappointment he heard? He held the keys, the steel catching the overhead light.

"Well. Good work today," Emerald stated after a moment's silence.

"You too." He grinned. "You earned a lot of points with the owner for letting out the dogs. Billings wouldn't let anyone go back in and let them out to the yard."

"Billings is a moron," she spat. "You don't think we're in for a rash of bombings now?" Emerald shifted closer.

Stx recalled the note he'd removed. He hoped not. "Job security," he quipped.

She barked a mirthless laugh. "You have a sick sense of humor."

He shrugged, hitting the locks. They clicked and the horn chirped. "We'll probably be in for some extra training."

Emerald nodded. "No doubt about that. Well, see ya."

Stx slid behind the wheel of his F-150 and watched Emerald speed walk away into the dark. Emerald was nice and even attractive. But he didn't go for the hard-eyed cop type. And he didn't want the complication of mixing work and pleasure. Plus, the department frowned on fraternization. He preferred the soft mocha-skinned woman with sad eyes and a sharp tongue.

Shortly after, Stx pulled in the drive of a large two-story home not far from an elementary school. He glanced around the residential neighborhood. Discarded bikes and balls littered some of the lawns. The yard he parked next to needed its hedges trimmed, but it did not contain toys or other child paraphernalia. Stx hopped out of the truck, grabbing a small bouquet and the bag of Chinese food he'd purchased on the way. His footsteps scuffed on the walkway. He mounted the steps and pushed the doorbell.

At the chime, August set aside the book she'd been reading to Isaac. She skimmed her fingertips lightly over the little boy's face. His eyes were closed, and his deep, even breathing signaled he'd fallen asleep. She smiled, leaned over, and placed a kiss on his forehead. She loved this little boy. She turned off the light and closed his door on her way out.

The doorbell pealed again. Frowning, August hurried down the half flight of stairs and into the downstairs foyer. Who could be visiting at this hour? Hopefully, there was nothing wrong with any of her neighbors. She pressed the intercom next to the door.

"Yes?"

"Sol. It's Stx."

August pressed a hand to her heart. *What was he doing here?* She twisted the deadbolt, removed the chain, then turned the knob. The cool night air blew the scent of musk and burning leaves. Before she could say a word, Stx engulfed her in his strong arms and surrounded her with the scent of musk and man.

"I've never been so scared in my life," he murmured.

August clung to him, giving herself over to being held. How many times that day had she been on the verge of tears? It could've been her last day on Earth. She'd even read an extra story and given Issac a second snack because she was so grateful to be alive. And now this man, one she barely knew, was holding her as if she were his very life.

"I couldn't wait for our date." He closed the door with his foot.

August swallowed the lump in her throat. "We hardly know each other," she muttered.

"C'mon, August, we've known each other a very long time." He walked her backward until her back rested against the wall. "Had you married me when I asked, we'd be sitting on a beach making love."

He seldom called her by her given name, and the syllables drifted over her like a minky robe. She clutched at the front of his shirt. "We were too young, and you were too reckless."

He stared down into her face a brief moment before his lips covered hers. "Instead, you married a man who broke your heart and trust," he scoffed.

"Why are you here?" she demanded, tearing herself from his arms.

He pulled her against him.

"I'm here because I refuse to allow another day to go by without telling you how I feel."

"Well, kissing me senseless isn't going to help," she snapped.

He chuckled. "It used to."

"I've grown up, Samson. I'm still raising a child. I can't allow hormones to dictate my actions."

Once more, she found her back pressed against the wall and his mouth on hers. The sexual onslaught dissolved whatever argument she had. What was wrong with giving into hormones when they made her feel so good? What was wrong with indulging her desires with a man she'd never stopped loving? A man who still held a torch for her. For her!

She yanked his shirt from his waistband, needing skin-to-skin contact. He sighed when she touched him. She skimmed her fingertips across his taut muscles and washboard abs and traced his tangled, curly chest hair that disappeared into his jeans.

How many times had she followed that trail to the erection straining at his zipper?

"I love you, August. I never stopped."

Tears burned her eyes. "It takes me nearly getting blown up for you to realize you love me," she muttered thickly.

He chuckled. "I want a family, and I want it with you."

She shook her head. "I can't have anymore kids," she whispered. "Several years ago, I had to have an emergency hysterectomy. No more babies."

He cupped her cheek with such gentleness that her eyes spilled with tears.

"Then we'll raise Isaac together."

Chapter Six

S tx cupped the soft weight of Sol's breasts in his hands, relishing the sigh easing from her lips. "Tell me you want me."

"Of course I want you."

"Is your room upstairs?"

Taking his hand, she skirted the stairs, led him down a short hall, and turned right. He had enough time to marvel at how she led him through the darkened house without mishap. They passed through a living room, the furniture in shadow. Another door was on his right, but she kept moving toward the open door next to the brick fireplace.

Stx sank into the plushness of the thick carpet that muffled his footsteps. He closed and locked the door. He could make out the uncertainty on her face in the pale moonlight. Had he moved too fast? She still held his hand, and it trembled in his. No, he needed this. They both needed to know they were alive.

He tugged her off balance, catching her to him. "I want all of you." He kissed her, exploring her mouth, dueling with her tongue for supremacy. He teased her nipples, realizing she wore no bra.

He glanced down her body; she wore a cotton night-shirt that skimmed her knees. Did she still have on panties?

Stx scrunched the material in his hands, slowly raising the hem. He lowered to his knees as he pushed the gown higher. The scent of her arousal beckoned. Sol placed a hand on his shoulder. He wasn't sure whether she intended to push him away, but he wouldn't allow that.

He shoved the gown a little higher, baring her dewy nether lips. He leaned close, blowing a stream of his warm breath against her most sensitive parts.

Above him, she quivered. How hard would she shake if he pressed a kiss there? There was only one way to find out.

He teased her damp folds. Enjoying how responsive and wet she was for him. He flicked his with tongue over her slit, enjoying a long, slow lick.

August held her breath. Every bit of saliva in her mouth dried, and all she could do was moan in pleasure. Why had she waited so long to do this? Goobers and raisins, she couldn't even remember the last time she'd had sex. Did she still know how? "Oh, Samson," she hissed when Samson slid one long finger inside her as he continued eating her out. She moved her hips in time to his marauding mouth. He eased in a second finger, thrusting in and out. There was no way she could hold out against his foreplay. Before she realized it, she was sliding into her first orgasm

August gasped, barely biting back the shriek of pleasure gurgling in her throat. Before she could recover, Samson lifted her nightshirt over her head and carried her to the bed. He laid her gently on the bed. She reached for him, and he deftly stepped out of her reach.

Even as he shed his clothes, he took every opportu-nity to fondle and maintain Sol's state of arousal. When he finally settled between her legs, August had a sense of coming home.

Stx eased into her tight folds. God! She was so tight, and he didn't want to hurt her. She twined her legs around his, pressing her pelvis upwards, urging him on.

"Don't stop," she pleaded.

"We have the whole night." He grasped her hips, enjoying the constriction. He released a slow grateful sigh when he slid balls deep. He needed a moment. Even with the condom, he needed to breathe to keep from cumming too soon. He hadn't expected her to be so tight. He bent his head and captured one hard nipple between his teeth. He bit down gently. When she gasped, he laved the tip.

She always liked a little bit of pain with her pleasure. He did the same thing to her other breast. His cock was bathed in her heat.

He moved slowly, taking his time as he withdrew, then entered again. He kept his thrusts slow and deliberate, watching the wonder and awe play across Sol's face. He loved watching the emotions skitter over her features. She gripped his sweat-slicked biceps, trying to get him to move faster.

"This is one of those slow songs with precise syncopation." He punctuated his words with a hip grind. "There's no need to hurry when loving you is this good." He hooked an arm beneath one of her knees, and he slipped a little deeper. With his other hand, he pinched her nipple, then rolled the tight bud between his thumb and forefinger.

"Oh sweet Jesus," she breathed, arching her back.

The king-sized bed bounced with their movements, and the headboard kept in rhythm. August gripped a handful of the sheets with one hand and Samson with the other.

There was no way she could last through this. Her body was already coiling for another release. And all she wanted him to do was hurry his pace. No matter what she did to make him move faster, he drove her wild by keeping the same careful beat. He flexed his hips, hitting just the right spot. She slid into a sweet and long climax that made her forget how to breathe. She clung to his heavier body, her only anchor in a sea of pleasure. A few moments later, he fell beside her, panting.

Briefly, he rolled away, and when he returned, he gathered her in his arms.

"You are even better than I remembered." He traced the outline of her lips. He squeezed her hard. "I'm so glad you're okay."

She squeezed him back. "What do we do from here?"

He reached under the pillow and rolled on another condom. "I'm going to make the best of our night together."

Stx didn't bother to hide his good mood the following morning. He and Sol had not slept much the night before. He'd been intent on relearning every curve and valley of her body. He smiled at the memory of rediscovering the little spots that made her moan. The spot just behind her ear or the spot on the back of her knee. And she'd even made him breakfast before he left.

"Well, you look like a man who has been laid," a voice sneered.

Stx turned to find Detective Hank Potter leaning against the wall. Stx studied the other man a moment. The normally florid complexion he'd associated with Potter was no longer there. The gel-spiked hair and arrogant tilt of his head were still present.

"How was rehab?" Stx asked pleasantly. "Gotta say your breath smells much better now."

Potter's dark eyes narrowed. "Shut your mouth. You have no idea what you're talking about."

Stx quirked an eyebrow. "Oh? About rehab or your breath?" Stx reached in his pocket, removed a package of gum, and flicked it in Potter's direction. "Maybe it's the breath."

Potter caught the package.

Stx resumed whistling and walked toward the locker room. He paused with his hand on the door and looked over his shoulder. Potter was staring daggers at him.

"I heard you're working with us on this investigation. Have you learned anything, Hank?"

Hank sneered. "It's my investigation. I don't need your help."

Stx flashed a mirthless smile. "Right. Next time there's something that goes boom, call someone else." He finished pushing open the door and walked through.

⌒

"Come!" August commanded. She laid a closed fist just above her right knee. A cold, wet nose bumped her hand. She grinned. "Good boy. Sit."

An energetic jingle of tags signaled that the dog had complied. Again, August praised the animal. "Now stay." She held her open hand down, palm out. She backed away slowly. A flash of yellow and a pink nose filtered through her vision. Her guide's alertness filled her with awe.

August loved animals, but she especially loved dogs. Dogs were a bit like people. They both came in all shapes and sizes, but dog and man differed because the canine loved no matter what. Just pure unconditional love.

"Take a break!" She stooped petting, praising, and scratching the dog behind his ears, then beneath his chin. "Such a good boy."

With a smile, she straightened. She felt a twinge of pain and soreness radiating from certain intimate parts of her body. She bit back the gooey smile at the activities that caused the pain and soreness. Stifling a wide yawn, she walked to Riley's water bowl and filled it. Once she heard slurping, she went back to her thoughts. She hadn't got much sleep last night. Goodness, she couldn't remember the last time she'd spent the night making love. And that's what it had been. Samson used the hours of the night to love her so thoroughly that she knew she wouldn't be able to walk away from him no matter what her head told her.

A door slammed. Running footsteps preceded the slide of the patio door.

"Hi, Mom!" Isaac greeted, wrapping his arms around her waist.

She turned in his hug, bending to kiss his cheek. "How was school today?"

The little boy sighed dramatically.

August bit back a smile. "That bad?" Knowing the little boy was fond of nonverbal cues. she rested a light hand on his head.

He nodded. "Michael wouldn't stop yelling," he explained in his lisping voice. "Then he, then he ran around the room knocking off everybody's papers from their desks.

Ms. Babinger had to call his mother to come and get him. It was a horrible day," he said seriously.

"My goodness. It sounds like Michael had a very horrible day."

"Oh yes. We even tried to help, but Miss Tracy led us into the hall so Ms. Babinger could calm Michael."

"Do you have homework?" she asked, reaching for his backpack.

A heavy sigh was her answer.

"Go change your clothes, and we'll sit down and do your homework."

Hand in hand, they walked toward the sliding patio doors. "C'mon, Riley," she called. Jingling tags and panting signaled the dog's arrival. August stepped aside to let the child and animal go first. She locked the door as Riley tipped in one direction and Isaac in another.

She was loading Isaac's homework in the scanner when her phone rang.

She pulled the device from beneath her bra strap. "Hello."

"Good afternoon. I hope this isn't a bad time," a male voice greeted.

August ran through the list of voices trying to place the caller. "David?"

"Yes. I was calling to see how you're doing? If you needed anything, 'cause you know I got your back."

"Oh. Thanks. I'm fine."

"Oh. Yesterday was pretty scary."

"It was," she agreed. "Thankfully, no one was hurt. Thank you again for getting me out of there."

His smile came through loud and clear. "Anytime. Maybe we could have dinner?"

Even if the bomb hadn't been deadly, the man had saved her life. "I suppose I could do that as a way of thanking you. I'm sure the guy I'm dating now won't mind."

Silence.

She tilted the phone away from her face. A voice announced the phone number and length of the call. "Hello? Are you still there?"

"Oh. Yes. I didn't know you were dating anyone." Had his tone grown colder, or did she imagine the change? "I thought you didn't have anybody special."

"Mom, can I have something to eat?" Isaac called, running into the kitchen.

"Just a sec, I'm on the phone." She walked into the kitchen as Isaac opened the fridge door. "I'm sorry, David. This isn't a good time."

"Oh yes. Of course. Call me later?"

"Bye." August disconnected the call, then stuck the device back in her bra strap. "All right, kid. What are you after?"

"A salad."

"All right. Get what you want on your salad," August told him, moving to the cabinets to grab a small bowl and fork.

The fridge door opened and slammed a few times before all the salad ingredients were on the counter.

"What's for dinner?" Isaac asked, dropping a couple of cherry tomatoes on his salad greens.

"Spaghetti." The phone vibrated against her skin. "Message from Samson," an Australian accented male voice announced.

August grinned. She dug in her back pocket for her earbuds. Little ears didn't need to hear everything. She plugged one of the buds into her right ear and waited for the chime to signal her phone was now through the earpiece.

"From Samson. You rocked my world. I can't wait to spend more time with you. I meant what I said. I want you for the long haul."

True to his word, Stx spent every available moment getting to know Sol and her son. One chilly Sunday afternoon, they nursed cups of hot chocolate as Isaac stood on a wooden bridge tossing handfuls of breadcrumbs into the water. Huge carps, large-mouthed bass, and a few other species broke the surface to gather the treat. The child's delighted laughter rang through the silent trail.

"I can see why you made the choice to raise him. He's a ball of energy, and he's so smart."

"I love him fiercely. But there are times I feel like a total failure. When my other kids were his age, I could help them read, write, and teach them colors. With my vision the way it is now, I feel like he's being short-changed. Most of the time, I make up stories to tell him. We've done so many renditions of 'The Three Little Pigs.' It's hilarious."

"Is that his favorite story?"

"One of them. 'The Little Red Hen' and 'Three Billy Goats Gruff.' Sometimes all of those characters will make an appearance in one story."

Stx laughed. "I'd love to hear that sometime."

"Bet you would." August sipped her drink. "Has there been any progress on who sent the package to me?"

Stx stared after Isaac. "Be careful," he called.

Isaac turned and waved before going back to tossing breadcrumbs.

"What's he doing?" August asked anxiously.

"He's fine," Stx chuckled. "He was trying to climb the fence." He squeezed her fingers. "I promise I won't let anything happen to him."

August nodded. "Okay."

Stx wrapped an arm around her shoulders and pulled her close. For a moment, she resisted before settling into him. "You always do that."

"Yeah, you would too if you got snapped at for cuddling," she stated dryly.

"Your ex didn't like to cuddle?"

"Remember when I said my marriage got complicated toward the end?"

"Yes."

"We decided to try an open relationship. The female he chose was the same girl he'd been rolling around with for years. I didn't realize it at the time. By the time everything came out, I'd had enough." She sighed. "I didn't mind the open relationship. I'll admit it was fun especially knowing I didn't have the entire responsibility for making him happy. What I didn't like was her making snide comments that two queens can't exist in the same house, or oh my god he always seems like he's sleeping on top of you."

Stx studied her face. Sadness and grief clung to her features. "So you wouldn't be interested in a wholly monogamous relationship?"

She slipped her free arm around his waist. "I'm very interested in what we have here and now," she responded truthfully. "You know I was fairly adventurous."

He nuzzled her ear. "Does that mean you're open to threesomes or a little pain with our pleasure?"

"If you ever wanted a threesome, I wouldn't be opposed."

Stx paused as lust so hot and violent sent blood rushing to his cock. "You can't say things like that and not expect me to react." He stepped behind her, pressing his erection firmly into her buttocks.

"Samson!" she admonished, trying to pull away.

He held her in place. "Oh no. You're going to stay put until it goes down."

She laughed, a sound so carefree it squeezed his heart.

"We are in public!" she gasped between giggles. "In a family-friendly environment."

"And I'm trying to keep it that way."

She laughed harder, nearly doubling over in her mirth. Her reaction only served to press her buttocks into his bulging erection.

Stx groaned. "Woman, you're killing me!"

"Mom. Mom." Isaac ran up and grabbed her hand. "Can I have some more bread?" He stopped. "Hey. What's so funny?"

"Did you say more bread?" August asked.

"The fish are still hungry." He bounced up and down. "They like when I feed them."

"Show me," she urged, allowing the little boy to lead her to the wood railing. She glanced over her shoulder, a smile on her lips. "Bring the rest of the bread, Samson."

"Oh, you're not getting away that easy," he muttered.

A thrill raced down her spine at the promise of retaliation in his voice. "We're on a family outing," she teased.

Stx fished a small bag of breadcrumbs from the bag slung over his shoulder. He passed it to Isaac. "We are enjoying a family outing." He stood next to her at the rail. She leaned into him with a contented sigh.

This was the first time she'd initiated contact and simply melted into him. His heart did a stutter step. He rested his head on the top of her head as he stared out over the water. This was the best day of his life.

"I want this for the rest of our lives, August. I know we haven't been together long, but I know this is right. You and Isaac are where I want to be."

Beside him, August stiffened. "Samson."

"Now, don't go jumping to conclusions." He reached into his jeans pocket and pulled out a ring.

She backed away. "I couldn't."

Stx caught her hand. "You didn't let me finish." He grabbed her left hand and gently pushed the ring on her third finger. "It's a promise ring with sapphires and diamonds. This is my promise that when you're ready, I will marry you."

She stared at him, eyes overwrought with unshed tears.

"I know you've been hurt really bad in the past. Whether it takes five days, five years, or the rest of our lives, I promise to love and cherish you as the perfect gift you are."

A single tear slipped down her cheek. "And if I never want to marry?"

He placed her hand on his cheek, his smile evident. "As long as I'm with you, my world is complete."

Chapter Seven

"We've had another one of those confetti bombs," Emerald said.

Stx settled his goggles into place. "How many does that make now?"

"Eight."

He pulled on latex gloves and walked to the table with the dissembled bomb. He glanced at Emerald as she donned her own protective eyewear and gloves. "Where was it found?"

"Outside of Kerrytown, downtown where they normally have the Farmer's Market."

Stx frowned. "Why there?"

He set down the piece of wire he'd been examining and pushed his goggles up on his head as he walked toward a large wall map of Ann Arbor. Colored pushpins marked various points around the city where a bomb had been found. The locations were spread all over the city. Stx reached up, selected a blue pin, and pressed it into the map near the Farmer's Market. He stepped back to scrutinize the map.

The first two bombs, which found their way to the pet groomers and Sol's training facility, were close together.

Three and four had been found at a local grocery store and a nearby library. A fifth was found at a park. The sixth was on a nature trail near the U of M, and the seventh was at an ice cream shop. And the eighth?

His gaze snapped back to the seventh pin. Ice cream?

Cold fear sliced through his veins, turning his legs to jelly and his gut to water. "No," he breathed in horror.

"Stx?" Emerald queried.

He must be overreacting and reading more into what he saw than was warranted. But he'd taken Sol and Isaac for ice cream at that shop. They'd walked the trail and fed the fish. The park was one he knew Sol took Isaac to regularly. It was a few blocks from her home. And they were supposed to visit the Farmer's Market this weekend.

"Hey! What's going on? Are you all right?" Emerald hurried to his side as he swayed.

"Where's Potter?" He pushed away from her as she tried to steer him to a nearby chair. "I need to speak to Potter."

Emerald stepped in front of him, blocking his path. "You'll speak to me first. You've gone pale, and that's not a good look on a black man."

Stx drew in a jagged breath. He had to get control of himself. He forced another breath. All right. The earlier panic was receding. When he refocused, he saw concern and genuine fear on Emerald's face.

"The confetti bombs are all at places associated with Sol or where I've taken her."

Heavy banging reverberated on the front door. August swore as Riley emitted a sharp, startled bark. She placed a hand on her pounding heart as Riley nudged her knee.

"Scared me too, boy," she admitted. "Let's see what's so urgent." She rose from the sofa as the pounding continued. "Hold your horses!" she hollered. "I'm coming!"

Once she made it to the door, she pressed the intercom. "Who is it?"

"It's the police, ma'am. We need to speak with you."

Fear guided her actions, and she threw open the door. "What is it? My kids?" she demanded. "Has something happened to my children?"

"Your children are fine," the man told her.

A new fear clawed at her insides. Samson! Something had happened to Samson. She gripped the wood frame of the door. "Samson?"

"I told you to wait for me!" another male voice snapped. This one was deeper and older. The man rushed past and gripped Sol by the elbow. "All is well, Ms. River. Your Samson is fine. He sends his regards and will see you as soon as he leaves the lab."

August sighed in relief. Her legs would no longer support her, so she backed up and plopped on the bottom step. She dropped her head in her hands, breathing deep to calm her overwrought nerves.

"Potter, you need to work on your people skills," Sgt. Falls admonished.

"Potter?" August repeated. "Detective Potter?"

"Yes, ma'am."

"Then you must be Sgt. Falls," August said.

"Yes. I apologize for my partner's lack of empathy. He's a work in progress."

"And all of my loved ones are safe?" she asked anxiously.

"Yes, ma'am," Falls answered.

"Ms. River," Potter began with a gentle voice, "I truly did not mean to upset you."

Despite the clipped and hesitant apology, she did hear sincerity in the man's tone.

"We're following up on a lead and wanted to ask you a few questions."

"About?"

Potter closed the door. "If you would be more comfortable, we could speak in the living room."

Her thoughts were so jumbled. She had just realized she was sitting on the steps and stood up. "Yes, the living room would be more comfortable." She led them down the short hall. She resumed her place on the sofa, her guide settling at her feet. A moment later, she heard her guide chewing on a toy.

The sofa dipped on the other end. "Could you tell us what places you visit?" Sgt. Falls prompted.

"You mean like where I shop or go during any given day?"

"Yes."

August frowned. "But what does that have to do with anything?" She paused as she thought through the question. "Another bomb was found?"

"Yes?"

"Where?" she demanded.

Potter glanced at Falls, who nodded. "It was found at the Farmer's Market downtown."

August was silent. She'd been following the news, and though Samson had told her very little about the investigation, she knew he was concerned. From the news, she knew another bomb had been found on a trail she often used. It was the same trail where Samson had given her his promise ring. She fidgeted with the band, turning it round and round on her finger.

"You think someone is after me?" she asked quietly. At the moment, the scenario didn't seem real. Who would want to hurt her? She barely knew anyone in the city. Had she picked up a stalker or had some other crazy fixated on her? "I've only been in Ann Arbor the last few years. Before that, Ohio."

"But you go to these places?" Potter pressed.

"Yes, at least once a week." She dragged her fingers through her locs. "We, my six-year-old and I, always try to do something on the weekends. There's a park we go to a few times a week when the weather's good. We walk various trails around the city, go for ice cream, or stock up on Kinder eggs."

"Kinder eggs?" Potter repeated.

"They're a chocolate egg which hides a small toy inside. Kids love em," Falls answered.

"Oh," Potter responded. He shifted on the couch. "Is there anyone who would want to hurt you?"

"If my ex and his wife were still alive, I'd say his wife would," she retorted. "But I can't think of anyone." She waited for a beat as a thought occurred. "What about that guy? Um. Mr. VIP? Wasn't he targeting small business owners and people with disabilities?"

"We checked," Falls assured her. "He is safely ensconced in jail. He's in solitary for his own protection."

"What about Stx? Could someone be using these bombs to get to him?" Potter asked.

"What do you mean?"

"How well do you know Stx?" Potter continued.

"We went to school together. You think someone is after Samson and using me to do it?"

"You would be a weak link."

"Because I'm blind?" she demanded with enough frost to crack ice.

"Because you wear his ring," he pointed out. "He's had some pretty bad breakups."

"I see." She stood, signaling the end of the interview. "Detective Potter, I hope you're a better investigator than you let on because your people skills suck."

Falls coughed to cover a snort of laughter. "We appreciate your time, Ms. River. If you get any unexpected packages, don't open them."

August followed them to the front door. "No worries about that. I'm being extra careful."

Once the two men left, August locked the door. She had to talk to Samson. Who would want to hurt either of them? She pulled out her phone and pressed the side button. When it chimed, she said, "Text Samson."

"What do you want to say?"

"Call me as soon as you can. The detectives were here. They think someone could be targeting me to get to you."

The phone repeated her message, then added. "Are you ready to send?"

"Yes."

A swoosh filled the silence. "It's sent."

A few minutes later, the doorbell rang. It was time for August to go to work. She clicked her tongue for Riley. The yellow lab darted to her, eager for the leash and harness. She then left the house, pausing long enough to hit the bottom middle button on the keypad to lock the door. The lock whined and slid into place.

The wind blew a hint of burning leaves and a whiff of familiar cologne. August sniffed but was unable to place the scent. As she entered the bus, allowing Riley to guide her up the three short steps, she pondered who would want to hurt her. She couldn't think of anyone.

⌒

"That Potter guy is such a jerk," Sol told Stx over dinner a few days later.

Stx patted her hand. "I know."

"He thinks someone is using me to get to you, and he mentioned your personal life."

Stx sipped his water. The last couple of days had been a blur of activity. He hadn't been able to see her the night Falls and Potter visited because he got stuck on a call. Then there was training over the next day and a half. Between her schedule and his, this was the first evening they'd been able to sit down and eat as a family.

He stole a look around the table. Isaac was shoveling corn and mashed potatoes in his mouth as though someone would snatch his plate away. Sol pushed the portion of grilled chicken around on her plate, and a TV blasted the theme song to "PJ Masks." Stx realized even more than ever how much he wanted a family. The last few weeks of them dating was the most at home he'd ever felt in a relationship. Sol didn't nag him about the time he was away. Instead, she often left messages on his phone for him throughout the day.

The sadness he'd first seen on her face was long gone. She seemed more settled and happier. He glanced at the ring on her finger. She hadn't taken it off since he'd given it to her.

He hoped that was a good sign. Sol still hadn't mentioned marriage, but he was content to spend whatever time he could with her regardless.

"When I'm done with this training, how about we take off for the weekend?"

"Let me check my schedule. I know I've got classes this weekend, but I'm sure I can get someone to cover."

"Do that. And we can leave right after Isaac is out of school."

She grinned. "He doesn't have school on Friday. Tomorrow is his last day for the week."

"Even better. We'll take a few days and relax. We could visit the Point for their Halloween Spooktacular."

"I haven't been there in years," August said. "Let's do it."

Stx grinned. That was the answer he was hoping for. He had no doubt August was the right woman for him. He stood, came around the table, and cupped her cheek.

"What is it?" August asked.

"You're the best thing to ever happen to me. Always remember that."

She gripped his wrist. "I've learned to live in the moment. No matter how scary something is or uncertain, especially with your career choice, it's best to live in the moment. The next moment isn't promised."

He pressed his lips to hers, not knowing how true her statement would be.

Chapter Eight

S tx and Emerald stood side by side, examining a box of magazines. It wasn't so much the magazines but the small silver canisters duct-taped to either side of a brick of gray clay. Eight wires ran from the clay to the canisters, then to a large digital timer.

"What do you think they put in the canisters?" Emerald asked.

"Last time, it was green slime," he grimaced.

"All right, boys and girls. It's simple," a disembodied voice explained. "The first team to disarm the bomb wins. The losing team gets a little surprise."

Three other teams were in the room as well. "As long as it's not that stink bait crap," a man named Ingersoll quipped from the far end of the room.

"Be on the losing boom, and you'll find out."

Everyone else groaned.

Emerald looked at Stx, and Stx lowered his face shield. "This should be fun."

Emerald shook her head, trying not to smile. "Only because no one gets hurt."

"And go," the disembodied voice said.

Stx and Emerald approached their box. The other teams did the same. A couple of teams were stripping wires but not cutting them.

Emerald picked up a wire cutter. "C'mon. We're falling behind," she hissed.

Stx walked around the platform holding their makeshift bomb. Something about the wires and the timer didn't look right. He lifted his face shield, bending to take a closer look. He sniffed. "You smell that?"

Emerald lifted her shield and sniffed as well. "Yeah. What is that?" She inhaled deeper. "It smells a bit like almonds."

Stx frowned. "You think LT is using a different type of clay this time around?"

Wary now, Emerald moved one of the stacks of magazines aside.

A mild pop and curses filled the air. "Looks like Team Three is dead or has lost a few fingers."

Stx glanced to his left to find both Team Three members covered in a runny, beige substance the consistency of oatmeal.

"Well, at least we know what's in one of the canisters," he quipped.

They worked quickly but methodically. Once Emerald stripped the wires to reveal the metal beneath, Stx applied an alligator clip to bypass the triggering mechanism.

Neither breathed a sigh of relief until both canisters were rendered safe.

Stx lifted his face shield, then wiped the sweat from his forehead with the back of his hand. "For a moment, I thought LT had a sample of Explosive 808," he said.

"That's what it was!" she exclaimed. "I couldn't remember the name of the stuff."

"And time!" LT called.

"You all did good, except for Team Three, whose family I've had to inform there was an accident."

A few groans and chuckles went around the room.

"With this confetti bomber, we need to be vigilant. Up to now, the bombs have been harmless."

"And not expertly done," Nunez added under her breath.

"No. We don't know if someone is doing this for fun or if there is an actual message," LT continued. "All it takes is one to explode and hurt someone."

A faint hiss followed by a plume of smoke drew attention to the second table.

"Yo, LT?" Nunez called. "Is your experiment supposed to do this?"

Stx sniffed the air. Something like burnt motor oil filled the room. "What is that?"

Emerald, who was closest, stepped to the table. "Guys, this is a live bomb," her voice was deathly calm.

"How the fuck —"

A siren wailed, and the room went into lockdown. All earlier joking ceased. Boots clattered around the room as everyone pulled protective equipment from cabinets.

Someone maneuvered a robot into place.

Stx held up a bomb blanket as Emerald snipped and clipped wires.

"Get back, Emerald," Stx told her.

She shook her head. "Get back. I can defuse it before it blows."

"Thirty seconds," Nunez said.

Before the words left her mouth, an explosion from Team Three's device filled the room with smoke and noise. Stx barely registered the screams and curses as an even bigger bang lifted him off his feet and slammed him into a wall. Pain singed every nerve ending. He lifted his head, and the world went black.

⌒

"Where is he?" August demanded.

"I'm going to find out for you," DJ told her.

August swiped at the tears on her cheeks. This couldn't be happening right now, not when they'd made plans to go to Cedar Point and view the Halloween festivities.

"We're looking for Samson Denver," DJ told the woman at the information desk.

"Ms. River?"

August turned in the direction of the voice. "Yes?"

"It's Sgt. Falls. Come with me."

"How is he?" she demanded as Sgt. Falls led her to an elevator. "What happened?"

"The rest of the squad is trying to figure that out."

The elevator slid up. When the doors opened, murmured voices, the squeak of shoes on linoleum, and the scent of burnt coffee rolled in the air. Falls and August walked away from the noise. A door opened, and he led her inside.

"Wait here. I'm going to get Stx's Lieutenant."

Sol paced the small room. She was too keyed up to sit in one of the chairs.

"Mom, he's alive," DJ told her.

August nodded, not trusting her voice. She twisted the ring on her finger. Samson promised he wouldn't leave her, and like a fool, she believed him. She loved him fiercely. Even after she thought she couldn't fall in love again.

A knock preceded the door opening. "Ms. River?" a gentle voice asked.

"Yes?"

"I'm Lt. Barrett. Stx has you listed as his next of kin."

He did? When had he done that, and why hadn't he told her? She shook her head to dispel the thoughts. Now was not the time to get sidetracked.

"Please. What happened?"

Barrett took her hand and led her to a chair. "We're still sorting through that. There were eight in training today. I've never lost an officer during a training exercise."

Lost an officer? All of a sudden Barrett's voice was coming through a long, muffled tunnel. August nearly slid from her chair, but the Lt.'s strong arms kept her in place.

"Stx is alive," he told her firmly. "Do you hear me? Stx, Samson Denver is alive."

The knot tightening in her chest loosened, and she could breathe again.

"He's alive? He's alive?" she repeated. "You swear he's alive?"

"Yes, Stx is in surgery. His partner Emerald didn't make it. She took the brunt of the blast."

August ran through his words again. Samson was alive, but Emerald hadn't survived.

"Oh no. But what happened?"

"As near as I can tell, someone tampered with the devices, adding active ingredients beneath the training items. Stx suffered an injury to his head and eyes."

Someone was holding his hand. Stx tried to squeeze the fingers surrounding his, but he couldn't move. Why was his body so heavy? He shifted, and a host of aches and pains made themselves known. He moaned.

"Samson!" The hand tightened in his. "Oh, thank God."

He knew that voice. A sweet siren's voice. Was she crying? Why was she crying?

"Sol?" he croaked. "What's wrong?"

He coughed and wished he hadn't. Spasms of pain shot from his head to his chest and back again. Something plastic tapped his lips. A straw. He sucked the cool liquid. He hadn't known how parched he was until the first splash of water slid down his dry throat.

"Not too fast," she warned, pulling back the straw.

He tried to nod but couldn't move his head. He stretched his fingers and toes. His hands and feet were working. He tried to open his eyes. Nothing happened. He lifted a hand to his face. Thick bandages wound around his head and eyes.

"What is this?" he demanded.

Slender fingers enclosed his hand again.

"What do you remember?"

Remember? Images flooded his brain. The training. Sirens. Smoke. Noise. Pressure and heat as he went flying through the air.

"Somebody messed up," he muttered. "Emerald? What happened to her? Nunez and the rest? Are they okay?"

Silence.

"Sol?"

"Emerald didn't make it," she answered quietly. "The others suffered minor injuries."

"Why can't I move my head?"

"They want you to keep your head as still as possible. At least for a few days."

Stx strained to hear between the words. Something was wrong with him. Very wrong. "What aren't you telling me?" he demanded.

"The doctors—" her voice cracked. She cleared her throat and tried again. "There was some serious damage to the optic nerves. They couldn't save your left eye, and the flash burned your retina."

Stx went still. "What are you saying?"

Sol gently caressed his cheek before grazing her lips against his.

"You're blind, Samson. Completely and totally blind."

Chapter Nine

Now

"Go away!" Stx snarled.

"I will not!" Sol hollered back. She shoved the door.

Stx shifted his weight and managed to keep the door closed.

"There is nothing you can do," he said bitterly, resting one palm flat. His other hand held a gun, a semi-automatic Beretta.

There was no yip yapping of that ankle biter. Sol must have let the dog out. Now Stx could at least think. He touched a finger to his useless left eye, still not used to feeling the hollowness of his lost eye. They had fit him with a prosthetic one, but he seldom used it. Why give the appearance of sight when he had none?

He lifted the weapon to his temple. Full magazine. What was the best way to do this? Put the barrel in his mouth? Under his chin? Behind the ear? He had to be sure he did it right, or else he'd end up a vegetable.

He almost laughed. Even if he became a vegetable, he had a DNR, a do-not-resuscitate order in his medical file. He opened his eyes as wide as they would go, even touching his eyelids to be certain they were open.

Utter. Total. Darkness.

"So you're going to mope and fester in your room while your sister turns your house into a kennel?"

Why should he care what his sister did to the house? All he had the energy for was sleep. And even that reprieve was being stripped from him yip by yip.

"What difference does it make? I can't see it. I can't see anything." He said the last in a near whisper. Why couldn't Sol leave him in his despair? He didn't want to live in a world of darkness.

"But you can smell and hear," she shot back. She kicked the door.

Stx pushed all his weight against the wood. Why wouldn't she let him be? She had every chance to. It was bad enough that she never left his side in the hospital, but she wouldn't even leave him alone now.

Stx could no longer have the family he wanted and believed was his. And he couldn't protect the woman he'd pledged his love to. The partner who'd fought beside him.

The door bumped, and he pressed more firmly against it.

"I have nothing for you, August!" he spat. Even as he said the words, pain chewed at his heart with sharp, jagged teeth. The pain rivaled anything else he felt, and he immediately wanted to take back his statement.

"Because you lost your eyesight?" she demanded with such scorn that Stx forgot to hold the door.

When it opened an inch, he shoved back.

"So it's okay for me to lose my eyesight, but not you?"

He flinched. Sol wasn't yelling or screaming, which made her statement even worse.

"You don't understand," he muttered.

"You're right. I would never understand what it's like to not be able to see." She didn't hide the sarcasm in her voice.

"Go away, Sol," he pleaded. "Just leave me alone."

She thumped the door in response.

"Don't come back," he called.

"Tell your sister I'm taking her dog. This is the last time I clean up after her," Sol spat. "If she has a problem with that, tell her to sue me."

Stx slid down the door until his back rested against the wood. He cradled the gun in his lap. He'd wait until Sol was gone. He'd wait for the stupid dog to go. He'd wait until he knew the house was his again.

How did Sol and the other council members deal with this every day? They always seemed so happy. How did he live his life without sight? Without Sol? Without a family?

By slow degrees, the scent of bleach and pine permeated the air. Stx sniffed appreciatively. Even though he could still detect a hint of dog urine and feces, the smell wasn't as potent as before.

He listened to floorboards creak, cabinet doors slam, and water run for several minutes. The furnace hummed and clicked on. Warm air swirled through the room but did little to heat the chill in his soul.

He absentmindedly stroked the barrel of the weapon. A permanent end to a permanent situation.

Stx could recall every vivid detail of the training. The odor of almonds and motor oil mingled with fresh cordite. The mint of someone's mouthwash. The fresh scent of starch from their uniforms. He recalled his tension when he thought something was wrong with the device they'd been given. But their device was only a distraction. He remembered that Emerald had found a live bomb. And the explosion.

He touched the jagged scar above his left eyebrow. He had a nice piece of shrapnel to thank for his lost eye. How long he sat there, he didn't know. The house had long gone silent. Now and then, loud bass would vibrate the windows, but other than that, there was silence.

His stomach growled, and he ignored it. What was the use of eating? He didn't want to do anything that would prolong his life. Why hadn't he died in the explosion? He should've died in the explosion. Then he wouldn't have to live in darkness.

August shampooed the little dog for the third time. This time around, the soap lathered well. She ran her fingers through what had once been matted fur. How could someone treat an animal like this? She carefully rinsed the little dog, who pranced happily in place.

She stepped back when the dog shook off the excess water.

"Feels a lot better, huh, girl?" she asked. She again let the spray wash off the dog's body, making sure no soap remnants remained. August wrapped the thoroughly rinsed dog in a large fluffy towel. She rubbed the dog briskly, wishing she could rescue Samson as easily as she had this dog.

She didn't know how to reach Samson. Now that he had a clean bill of health, he was only going through the motions. His sister moving into his house, to "help him recover," August thought with a sneer, was not helping. The woman only made the situation worse

Samson had said some very hurtful things to her, but he was hurting. What bothered her most was she knew she could help him through this. He didn't even realize he didn't have to suffer alone.

Somehow Samson made her believe in love again. He made her believe in second chances and living to love each valuable moment. She touched the promise ring Samson had given her over a year ago. Would he break this promise too? Would she let him break this promise?

August set down the wiggling dog, who shook vigorously and took off running.

No matter what Samson's sister said or did, Sol would not be returning the dog. She'd foster the dog until she could find it a good home.

Her guide, Riley, whined. He had quietly sat while Sol bathed the little dog. Now, he was asking to play too. She unclipped his lead. "Take a break." Riley ran off.

Sol tossed the used towels in a hamper, cleaned the tub, then put away the shampoo and other bath items.

Sudden tears blurred her limited vision and dribbled down her cheeks. How dare Samson do this to her? To them? Didn't he realize she was suffering right there with him? Didn't he understand she was aching to show him how he could maintain his independence?

Here she was with an entire smart home. Everything from her lights and television to the microwave and dishwasher could start with a simple voice command. Even her doorbell camera announced when someone was at the door. Angrily, she swabbed at the tears. No. She wouldn't shed any more tears over him. If he couldn't see reason, she wasn't going to bother.

But life was so short. Hadn't she learned that? She knew what it was to love and lose and never tell that person that love was still there despite all the hurts. Hadn't leaving Richard Williams and his alternative lifestyle been one of the hardest decisions she'd ever made? Well, leaving Richard was easy as she hadn't felt he appreciated her and what she'd done for him throughout their marriage.

But she had mourned her daily life with Isaac. Daily video chats were not the same. Listening to the little boy cry because she wasn't home with him nearly destroyed her resolve to stay away. She loved that little boy with her whole heart, and now she was the only mom he had.

Just like Samson was the only anchor she had in this world. She'd believed him when he told her they'd spend the rest of their lives together. Well, not at first. But she gradually trusted that he would be there and be a father figure to Isaac. And now? Now she was alone again, raising her little boy. Alone.

"Damn you, Samson. Damn you for making me fall in love with you again."

Chapter Ten

"How long had he sat on the floor? Stx groaned as he shifted, his neck stiff from sleeping with his head propped between the door and the wall.

Quiet music filtered in from somewhere in the house. A faint feminine voice laughed, then spoke. He couldn't make out the words. He opened his eyes, seeking the bright red numerals of his digital clock. He couldn't see anything. Had the power gone out? Then he remembered. He was blind. He would never see again.

"Fuck it to hell!" he snarled. Stx placed a hand on the wall to assist him in rising and realized he still had the Beretta in his lap. Swearing again, he stood and stumbled toward the bed. He shoved the weapon beneath one of the pillows. Putting the gun back in the safe would be wasted energy. He needed to know the time. How long had he been asleep? Had his sister, Myrna, even checked to see if he was alive?

Stx stumbled back to the door and opened it a crack. Now he could hear her.

"Girl, I tell you. I haven't seen him this helpless in a long time. Mm-hmm." A pause. "No, he stays in his room all day."

Laughter floated to his ears. "I'm telling you, this is the best gig ever. Nah, he's got some blind lady friend who cleans a couple of times a week."

Stx edge the door wider. Who was she talking to? And where was she talking? He listened again.

"Oh. What about the dog? The one he gave me for my birthday?"

The hollow echo. Myrna was in the bathroom. How long had his sister been in the bathroom? He forced himself to think. She spent at least three hours a day in the bathroom. But was it morning or night?

"All I care is that the dog is quiet, and I ain't gotta hear her barking at every raindrop and snowflake that falls."

Stx stood on the threshold of his room. Anger roiled through him at her callous words. If Myrna wasn't here to help him, then why was she here?

"No, I just needed some time away from my family. You know my brother lets me do anything I want."

Stx marched toward the voice and ran smack dab into a wall. He ricocheted off and swallowed a curse. "Damn it!"

"Stx?" Myrna called.

"What?"

Breathing deep, he stopped, touched the wall, and tried to remember the layout of his house. He couldn't do this. He turned to go back to his room.

"Hey, Myrna," he called.

"You need something?" she called.

"Yeah. I need you to get your shit and get the fuck out my house."

Something clattered to the floor, followed by a toilet flush. Water ran for several moments before the door opened.

"What did you say to me?"

Stx glared in her general direction. "You heard me. Get outta my house."

"Of all the ungrateful—"

Finally, here was a worthy target for his anger and hurt.

"No, sis. You're the ungrateful one. You said you'd help me. You've done nothing but destroy my house with your caged dog and spend three hours in the bathroom. What do you do in there? If you're sitting on the toilet that long, maybe you need to see a doctor."

"But you need me."

"Need you?" he repeated. "You sit there and talk about me like I'm a dog. You talk about my lady friend as if she's some oddity or your maid. When's the last time you fed your dog? Or taken her for a walk?" he demanded.

"I—"

"Have you even noticed your dog isn't here?"

"What? What do you mean she's not here?" Myrna pushed past him.

Stx slowly followed, using the wall as a guide. He listened to her footsteps rush over the floor. He'd never noticed how heavy his sister walked until this moment. He could feel the house shake with every stride. Metal on metal scraped.

"Where's Coco?" She stood. Again the heavy tread. Doors opened and closed as Myrna called for the dog.

Stx listened and sniffed the air. He couldn't smell any trace of the dog. Whatever Sol had used left the air clean with just a hint of her lavender perfume.

A pang of regret washed through him. No. He wouldn't think of Sol. He wouldn't think of what he'd done. She wouldn't want him now. Not when he was broken and blind.

Heavy footsteps came toward him. "Where's my dog?" Myrna demanded. "Who cleaned this house?"

"You're my sister, and you don't have my best interests at heart. You wouldn't even have noticed your dog was missing if I hadn't said anything." He looked her up and down with as much contempt as he could muster. "You're not helping me, only yourself. Your dog is safe." He turned to retrace his steps.

She grabbed the back of his shirt. "Did you shoot my dog?" she demanded with a hint of fear.

"Thought about it," he replied pithily. "Sol has your dog. If you want it back, go talk to her." He jerked away from his sister and walked back to his room. He even managed to slam the door on her angry tirade.

After Myrna finished yelling and slamming doors, the house was finally quiet. Stx emerged from his room to survey the damage. He left his door open. What was he supposed to do now? He hovered on the threshold, turned back into his room, and reached for his gun.

Samson's house was way too quiet. Without the yapping dog to greet her, August cautiously unlocked the door. She glanced around the living room; vague shapes hunkered in the dimness.

The stench of unwashed man and spoiled food made her wrinkle her nose. A spurt of anger had her closing the door harder than she meant. She'd never had much patience. And she was upset that Myrna, who was supposed to be helping Samson as one of his supposed loved ones, wasn't doing anything but being a mooch. What had Sol expected when Myrna wasn't even caring for her dog?

And then there was Samson. Sol wouldn't be here if he had left her alone at that social event. She would still be in her protective bubble instead of losing sleep worrying whether he'd still be alive when she dropped in.

"Samson," she called.

With care, she made her way from the front foyer into the large spacious living room. She turned left at the open doorway, which led to a bathroom and two bedrooms. She made a quick right and stood outside a closed door.

Samson's body funk was more pungent here. He wasn't even bathing? She placed her hand on the knob, hoping he hadn't locked the door. If he had, it would give her a reason to kick the door down. Holding her breath, she twisted the knob. It opened easily.

She barely discerned the lump on the mattress. "Samson!"

The figure sat bolt upright. "What?"

"When is the last time you had a shower or changed your clothes?" she demanded.

"You're not my mother," he griped.

"And she wouldn't be proud of you either." August moved farther into the room and swept a squishy pile of clothes aside with her foot. She'd had enough.

"You think you're the only one who has suffered through this? I was fine until you walked back in my life. I was getting along great without a man to love." She fisted her hands on her hips. "You think it's so easy to get up every day and live in a sighted world? Well, it isn't! It's hard. I will never see my grandchildren's faces. That is, whenever I'm lucky to get them. I don't even know what Isaac's face looks like anymore. For that matter, I don't even know what I look like. Do you know why I used to ask you if I was coordinated? Because I can only see certain colors. Outside of those colors, I'm lost. Do you know why I'm so organized? Because I have to plan any trip outside the house. If I forget something at the store, I can't just jump in the car and go get it." She kicked aside a shoe. "Now that I have a guide dog, I have to deal with people wanting to pet him or talk to him, or a dozen other things people want to do when they see the dog and not the human attached to the other end of the harness. Do you think it was easy to get the call from your Lieutenant and pray you weren't dead? Then you accuse me of not knowing what it's like to be blind."

"Sol..."

"I know. You want me to go away and stay away. But you're going to hear what I have to say before I do. I'm tired of the men I love leaving me and me not getting my say. Dickey did that by getting himself killed. His wife did that when she decided to start an affair with him. To think I let the little hussy in my house when she was a teen. God, I was so stupid. But you, Samson, are going to listen. I love you. You knocked down all my defenses, and I fell in love with you again. You accepted Isaac as yours, and now I have to go and tell him you won't be around anymore. Every time I come over here, I wonder if I'll find you dead. Because obviously, that's what you want to be. You act like life stops because you're blind. The thing is you don't know how to live without vision. You were the life of the party as the Council for the Blind's sighted volunteer. It was fun and even cool to help the visually impaired navigate stores or hear audio descriptions at plays and other live events. Now that you have a chance to truly make a difference, you want to die. If you're going to kill yourself, do it now. Do it sooner rather than later because I'm tired of wondering if I'm going to stumble across your dead body."

She twisted off the promise ring and dropped it on the nightstand. "Now, I'll go away and leave you alone."

Stx couldn't move. His sleep-fogged brain was still trying to catch up with all Sol had said. He'd give anything to see her lovely mocha-skinned face with its full, lush lips and expressive eyes. Her tone told him she was scowling. But he heard something else. Sadness. No, the emotion was more pronounced than that. Grief. He heard grief. It wasn't the sadness he'd seen when they reacquainted. It was the grief of knowing you love someone and can't have them. A living death, a loss that would only intensify because you knew the person lived, and there was nothing you could do to be with the person. His Sol was grieving him.

He kicked at the tangle of sheets imprisoning his legs. Something brushed the bed, and the rustle of clothes and the scent of lavender stilled his movements.

The dull clink of metal on wood drowned out the beating of his heart. He never heard the front door close as he patted the nightstand for what dropped. His seeking fingers closed around the small ring, still warm from Sol's skin. He clutched the ring in his fist as his tears flooded.

Wasn't this what he wanted? To be left alone by everyone so he could off himself? So he didn't have to learn to live in darkness? So he could stay cloaked in trauma and despair?

"Yes," a small voice hissed. "This is exactly what you wanted." All Stx had to do was reach under the pillow. He shifted his hand, brushing the cool metal of his weapon. He recoiled so fast that he rolled off the edge of the bed, banged his head on the corner of the nightstand, and hit the floor hard. Pain shot from his forehead to the hip he landed on.

He pushed to all fours, banging his head again on the stand. This time hard enough to knock off the lamp and books on the surface. He batted them away.

"Sol!" he screamed.

He made it to his feet, bouncing from one wall to the next in his haste to leave his room.

His sister always led him from one room to the next. He slammed into a door and stubbed his big toe hard enough to crack the nail down to the quick.

"Dammit!" He punched a wall, his fist leaving a dent in the wallboard.

He hurried forward only to fall into the bathroom. He tripped over that stupid area rug and would've taken a header through the glass shower door if he hadn't caught the towel rod next to the sink.

This was ridiculous. He couldn't even make it from one room to the next in his own fucking house! Pathetic!

How many times had he marveled at Sol's ability to navigate her home? The first night he'd made love to her, she'd guided him to her bedroom without any lights on. Not once had she run into anything. And here he was in a house he'd owned for five years, and he couldn't get through it in the dark.

Panting, he dropped to his knees. The tile was cool and gritty against his skin. For the first time, he caught a whiff of his body. He wrinkled his nose at the fetid odor of grungy sweat socks and funky cheese. Was that his ass smelling like that? Enough dwelling in the pits of despair. If his partner Emerald could see him, she'd kick his ass.

"Seriously, Stx. I give my life, and you honor my memory by giving up?"

And Sol. He shoved the ring on his pinky finger. He got it as far as the first knuckle. When he was sure he wouldn't lose the ring, he stripped off his smelly clothes. He carefully felt his way around the bathroom. He had always kept a hamper in here. With one hand on the vanity and the other on the door, he tried to remember what the bathroom looked like before he lost his vision.

The vanity with the six-inch gap between the wall and the edge contained two fluffy hand towels. From the sink, he could locate the toilet and a wall with a window. If Stx put his back to the toilet and stepped forward, his hand brushed the cool glass door of the shower.

So if he was in front of the toilet and the shower was in front of him... Stx dropped his hand to find a basket of overflowing clothes.

A smile of triumph curved his lips. He dropped his dirty clothes on the pile. It was time to clean his body. After that, he would learn his house.

Chapter Eleven

August walked around the perimeter of the room with her guide, Riley.

"Good boy," she praised. She had a small class of about four dogs and their owners. She used Riley as a distraction for the other dogs to assist them with impulse control. One of the dogs barked, and she caught a quick glimpse of the pooch straining against the leash.

"Call her back and get her to focus on you again," August instructed. August made three more passes before she was satisfied the group had the lesson well in hand. "Go ahead and tell your dogs T-A-B."

She slipped a treat to Riley. "You've been such a good boy." She wiped her fingers on her jeans. As long as she kept busy, she didn't think about Samson. Two weeks had passed since she said her piece. Not checking on him, texting him, or calling him was the hardest thing she'd ever done.

"This class has been so helpful," a young woman said as she approached August. "Jelly here is so much better."

"I'm so glad to hear it. Same time next week?" August asked.

"Absolutely!" the woman agreed. "See ya."

A chorus of goodbyes filled the air amidst the tinkle of chimes.

"You are just so amazing," a male voice stated.

Excitement leaped through August before she realized it wasn't Samson's voice.

"Hi, David. I didn't think we had a class today."

"Oh, I just dropped by to see how you and Riley were getting along and see if you had time to grab a coffee," he said pleasantly.

August swept a wisp of hair from her face with the back of her hand.

"Tonight isn't good, but we could meet for coffee in the morning before my first class," she offered. With everything that had happened, she hadn't been able to thank David properly for his role in getting her to safety.

"Really?"

Even she could see and hear the wide grin in his voice. "Sure."

They settled on a place and time, which would be before she arrived at the dog center and after she'd dropped off Isaac at school.

"So, are you still seeing someone?" David asked as she straightened a stack of flyers.

A pang of regret filled her at his question.

"Why do you ask?"

"I noticed you weren't wearing your ring," he stated.

"It's being cleaned," she fibbed.

Some instinct warned her not to tell him the truth. She liked David and was appreciative of him saving her life, but he wasn't a man she wanted to date or get too friendly with. He had a clingy, needy quality that was a major turnoff.

"Oh. So, Stx is recovering well?"

"Yes." She bent over to grab more flyers from beneath the counter. She used the reprieve to steady her emotions. Discussing Samson was not a conversation she wanted to have with David. Why didn't he leave already? She paused. Something David said worried her, but she couldn't think what it was.

Fingers drummed above her.

"Well, I gotta run. Can't wait to see you tomorrow," David said.

"See ya," she called from her crouch.

The bell tinkled, signaling he'd left. She straightened with a handful of flyers. These she added to the stack on the counter. Mindlessly, she walked around picking up stray toys, then readied the food and water bowls for tomorrow's class, and then stopped. How had David known to call Samson Stx? She seldom referred to Samson by his nickname. A fissure of unease slid down her spine. Maybe she shouldn't have agreed to coffee.

Stx marveled at how much he'd learned. In two weeks, he had learned every inch of his house. Now he was thankful for the bump dots and the tiny strips of felt on various start buttons on appliances. Sol must have done this in some of her earlier visits.

Regret slumped his shoulders. He'd hurt Sol when he promised he wouldn't. He touched the ring at his throat. He placed it on a necklace so he wouldn't lose it. He kept it in some vain hope he could return it to her. If he were really honest with himself, he missed Sol. He missed her so much that some nights it hurt to breathe.

After he learned his house, he was determined to be better. That had prompted a call to Abigail, who promptly called Jethro, and Jethro, in turn, referred Stx to a mobility specialist named Mike. Mike was great. He walked the neighborhood and various other places with Stx.

Stx maneuvered through the living room to the closet near the front door. Today, he and Mike were going to tour Abigail's Place.

The accordion doors slid open noiselessly, and Stx retrieved his heavy jacket. He reached up to the shelf above and grabbed a collapsible cane. The first time he'd held the cane, it seemed foreign. Now, he couldn't imagine leaving the house without it. The cane had become his lifeline.

At a faint beep beep beep, Stx opened the front door. It was Mike.

"I never realized there were patches of rough tape on the floor," Stx marveled some forty-three minutes later. He walked back and forth, feeling the texture of the floor change beneath the soles of his shoes.

"I would help serve when we didn't have enough help, so the tape on the floor was a way we came up with to help me," Abigail explained. "Most still don't realize why the tape is there, if they notice at all."

"I really appreciate this," Stx said, his voice suddenly thick with emotion. "I really do."

Footsteps scuffed on the floor as Abigail drew near. "I'm really glad you're here, Stx. We've all been pulling for you."

"How do you do it?" he asked.

"Do what?"

"Not being able to see?"

"Everybody is different. I was born this way. All I can see anymore is sunlight and what colors I was able to see are now shades of gray. I've never seen faces or anything like that. Others in the Council have never seen anything at all, while some like you have had their sight snatched from them overnight." Abigail touched Stx's arm. "But you asked how do I do it? One day at a time. We face unique challenges, like not being able to see or not knowing when we need help. We live in a world run for and by the sighted and well, for lack of a better word, normal people. But what's normal anymore?"

"But you're so happy," he pointed out.

She laughed. "I am, but if you look a little closer, some in the Council are not happy with their lot in life. They're not well adjusted to their condition. Rodney was one of those people. Ana was another."

Stx thought a moment. Rodney was probably the most extreme in his dysfunction. Ana just refused to use the technology at her fingertips, preferring to use what limited sight she had to read her phone screen instead of allowing the accessibility feature to read it for her.

"We have some very nifty things to help us maintain our independence, Stx," Abigail continued. "When is the last time you played the drums?"

"What?" The question caught him off-guard.

"You still play, right?"

How did he answer? He knew how to play the drums, or did he? Did he lose that skill as well as his eyesight?

"You haven't tried," she surmised.

He managed a self-deprecating laugh. "I guess I haven't."

"You know the biggest obstacle to living a full productive life is us." She gave him a gentle nudge. "Go try out the drums. They're still in the same place."

"Need a hand?" Mike asked.

Stx stood there a moment. A slow smile spread across his face.

"No, I think I got it."

He started toward the right side of the room, remembering the rough strips became shorter as they neared the stage. "But if I start to go off course, let me know."

Stx swung his cane back and forth with newfound confidence until he tapped something metallic. He explored the object with his cane before he finally determined it was the steps to the stage.

He mounted the three risers, pausing at the top to get his bearings. For the first time, he realized the stage sounded a bit hollow. He stepped forward, and the vibrations from his footsteps made the snare rattle.

Openness pressed around him, but sound deadened as he neared the drum set. His fingers brushed the high hat, making it trill. His heart leaped at the sound, and he touched each cymbal in turn. High hat, crash, and ride. Then the two toms, the floor tom, and the snare and bass.

He nudged the padded stool with his foot and felt an overwhelming urge to pour out his emotions. He folded his cane and sat.

Some of his best times were sitting behind the drums. He swept his hands over the floor tom and found the small stand of sticks. The smooth wood was so familiar in his hands. He tried a drum roll, and the snare sounded off. He dug in his pocket for his keyring and the drum key he always kept with him.

He went around the snare and tightened the squared spokes until he achieved the desired sound.

He placed the keys back in his pocket, inhaled a deep breath, and set a moderate 4/4 beat.

~

August stepped into Abigail's Place and stomped the snow from her feet. She loosened her scarf and unbuttoned her jacket as she got her bearings. She listened. Someone was on the drums, and they were pretty good. She adjusted the bag on her shoulder, then prompted her guide forward. As she crossed the room, the tempo changed to a frantic beat like something from an Imagine Dragons song. She wondered if Samson's band ever found a replacement for him.

"Abigail," August called out, hoping her voice carried over the music. She would not think about Samson right now. She continued down the corridor. Arriving at the bar when it wasn't open was always an interesting experience. The bar was open, but this was the lull before the night shift began.

Riley quickened his pace, and August knew Percy had to be nearby. Rough strips of texture met her shoes, and she was getting closer to the office. She knocked on the door.

"Come in."

August opened the door. "I won't keep you long. I wanted to drop off the blanket I finished."

"Wonderful!" Abigail exclaimed. She stood, crossed the room, and held out her hand.

August lifted the knit blanket from the bag and placed it in Abigail's hands.

"Oh, Sol, this is so lovely."

"I used the yarn you suggested, but it's a variegated shade of blue."

"I made Isaac one a few weeks ago, and I thought your grandson, Oscar, would like one too."

"Oh, thank you so much." Abigail hugged August. "I'll make sure he gets it."

"All right. I'll see you Saturday for karaoke."

"Good. What do you think of the drummer?" Abigail asked as they walked out of the office together.

"Sounds good."

"I thought so." She leaned close. "Have you heard anything from Stx?"

This was the question August feared. "No, and I really don't expect to." August didn't mean to sound so harsh, but she couldn't help it. Samson made her believe in love again. She'd said her piece, and now it was time to move on. "I know he suffered something traumatic, but he's not even trying. I can't watch him self-destruct."

"I understand. We each make our own choices," Abigail said.

August blinked back tears. "Thanks, Abigail. I'll see you Saturday."

Crash. Roll. Thump. Every cell in Stx's body drank in the beat he created. A freedom he hadn't known in months soared through him. He was playing! The music which seemed to have haunted his soul the past few months poured out as drum fills and rolls. Would his band still want him as the drummer?

The faint scent of lavender drifted toward him, and he faltered in the beat. The familiar scent conjured a curvy woman with sad eyes and full lips. The ache of not having her squeezed his heart, and he stopped, panting.

"...Saturday for karaoke, right?"

Stx raised his head. He knew that voice. His heart hammered in his chest. Sol was here.

"Yes. Any idea of what you might sing?" Abigail was saying.

In his haste, Stx kicked the high-hat cymbal, and it toppled to the floor with a loud clatter. He righted it, extended his cane, and searched for the stairs. He had to get to Sol before she left.

"Sol!" he called. He whipped the cane back and forth. It hit the air, and he paused, using his cane to poke for the steps. Where were they? A metallic clang. There. That was the handrail. He hurried down the three steps, scrubbed against the rough texture, and made his way to where the women were still talking. Apparently, neither had heard him call.

"I really need to go," Sol was saying.

"Sol?" he interrupted a bit breathlessly.

"Oh!"

"I'll leave the two of you alone," Abigail said and walked away.

Stx strained his ears for the retreating footsteps and heard a door close in the distance.

"I see you're not dead," Sol stated coldly.

He reached for her, and she stepped away. Disappointment filled him. She didn't even want to be touched by him anymore.

"Was that you playing?" Sol asked.

"Yes. I haven't played in months."

"There's a lot of things you haven't done in months," she countered bitterly.

He didn't need to see her face to hear and feel the hurt and anger rolling from her.

He took a deep breath and plunged in. "I'm sorry."

"For?" Suspicion colored her tone.

"In short, for being an asshole. Long story, for trying to give up on life and on love."

"Okay."

"I don't want to die, Sol. I just wasn't willing to live in darkness or figure out how to live in darkness. For me to say that it was okay for you and not me was a real shitty thing to say."

"Keep going."

"And once I stopped wallowing in my funk, I got my head on right."

"Good. I'm really glad you're doing better," Sol said sincerely.

"I know my way around my house and yard." He couldn't quite keep the note of pride from his voice. "I'm learning some new software. And let me tell you, Voiceover is a bitch to learn."

Sol laughed. "It is."

Stx drank in the quick laugh. It floated over him like a caress. "I miss you, Sol."

"Don't. Please don't. I can't." Her voice broke. She swallowed several times before she spoke again. "It's good you're learning to be a better blind person. At the end of the day, that's all we can do."

He was losing her again. He couldn't take it if she walked out on him again.

"Without you in my life, I would truly be in darkness," he spoke rapidly. "You placed bump dots and little felt strips on everything you thought I needed in the house. You did that while I was still recovering. The day you came in and read me the riot act, I realized I couldn't even run after you because I didn't know how to navigate my own house. How pathetic was that? Lived there five years, and I couldn't find my way to the front door." He shook his head at the memory. "You were right. I was being a coward and selfish."

Sol sniffled.

Stx wasn't trying to make her cry, but he couldn't let her walk away until she knew exactly how he felt. "I know I messed up. But I hope you can give me another chance." He stepped closer and touched her sleeve. She didn't pull away. "I need your sunny disposition in my life. I need your love, and I need you to call me on my BS."

Gentle fingers caressed his cheek. A sigh escaped his lips as he turned his face into her palm. How many nights had he dreamt of her touch? He held her hand in place before he kissed her hand.

"Oh, Samson," she sighed.

Stx pulled her to him and kissed her. For a moment, time stopped. They were the only two people in the world. She was sweeter than he remembered and a little thinner too. How could he have been so stupid to try and drive her away? He pressed his cheek to her damp one.

"Forgive me, August."

Cold air blasted in. "Mom! What's taking—Oh," DJ stopped. "It's about time."

August wiped at the tears on her face. "What's that supposed to mean?"

"You've been moping around the house the last few weeks."

"Have not."

"We can argue in the car. If we don't leave now, we'll be late picking up Isaac."

Stx wrapped an arm around Sol. "How about I come for dinner tonight?"

Sol placed a hand on his chest. "That would be really nice."

Stx held her hand there a moment before he lifted it, placed a kiss in the center of her palm, then closed her fingers over it. "Until tonight."

Chapter Twelve

Stx stood on the porch of Sol's two-story home. This was the first time he'd been to her house since the accident. He gripped the flowers in one hand and his cane in the other. He could do this. This was a familiar space and Sol would help him if he asked. He pressed the doorbell.

A moment later, the door opened, and a squeal of delight split the air. "Stx!" Isaac exclaimed. He grabbed Stx around the waist in a tight hug.

Emotion swelled and choked Stx as he returned the hug. "Hey, little man. I missed you," Stx told Isaac.

"Mom said you can't see anymore," Isaac told him solemnly. "She said you're just like her, and I should help when needed."

"Did she?"

"Uh-hmm."

"Come in already!" August called. "You're letting all the warm air out."

Stx maneuvered into the house and closed the door. The staircase was to his right and the hall to his left. He wiped his boots on the mat before taking them off and walking down the short hall in socked feet.

The floor was smooth wood. As he crossed into the living room, the floor changed to tile. He paused. How had he not noticed this before?

"Watch the table," Isaac cautioned. "It's here." He grabbed Stx's hand, dragging him until he placed his hand on the furniture.

"Thanks, little man." Stx remembered the table that sat at the edge of a large area rug next to one of the comfy chairs in front of the fireplace. Stx tilted his head at the crackle and pop. Sol had the fire going.

He sniffed the air. Something smelled good. If he wasn't mistaken, whatever Sol was making held a hint of garlic and rosemary.

"You can lay your coat on the chair. I'll get it when I come through there," August said.

Stx shed his coat and laid it on the back of the chair. He turned and made his way forward. Again the flooring changed, and he touched the back of a dining room chair. Now, he swung to his left. If he walked about three feet, there would be a high-backed bar stool.

The leather was cool beneath his seeking fingertips. He pulled out the chair, sat, and then folded his cane. A smile creased his lips. He did it! He managed to get his way around Sol's house from memory.

"Feels good, doesn't it?" She thunked a glass down near his right hand.

"Yes. You know what feels even better?" He wrapped his hand around the glass.

"What?"

"Knowing I have another chance with you."

August leaned against Samson, relishing the heat from the fire and the man next to her. She closed her eyes, inhaling his fragrance of sage and man. "I've missed you so much!' she admitted. "You don't know how many times I wanted to call or text or stop by to see how you were doing."

"I wanted to be mad at you, but I couldn't." He rubbed his chin on the top of her head. "How do you do it, Sol? How do you stay sane when you can't see?"

"I have good days and bad days," she admitted truthfully. "The good days are when everything goes right. I don't drop anything, and I remember where I set my cooking utensils. I don't run into anything, and people are kind and courteous." She stroked his cheek. "Bad days start as good days, but everything seems to go wrong. I misjudge a wall. Riley doesn't listen, or he gets distracted by a scent. I run into a wall, stub my toe, break a dish, and I blame it on my eyes. I get mad because I can't read the story Isaac really wants. I can't see his homework, or I have to ask for help filling out paperwork. Those are the times I wish the entire world could see like I do for a while, but then I wouldn't be unique. I appreciate the wind, the heat of the sun, the taste of chocolate, and how soft something is. Every day I live is a new adventure."

"So you think I'll have bad days too?"

"Absolutely." She snuggled closer. "Or maybe this past year will make up for all the bad days."

He released a quick chuckle. Yes, the last year had been bad, but it could be better. "I can't defuse bombs anymore. I'm retired and disabled."

"But you're not dead," came her quiet response.

No, he wasn't. He was very much alive. Sad he survived when his partner, Emerald, hadn't, but he was alive to live.

Yes, it sucked he'd lost an eye and his vision and he'd nearly lost Sol. He cinched her a little tighter. Even in his darkest moments, she'd been rooting for him to succeed for the simple reason she loved him.

She loved him in spite of what he'd lost. Loved him for the very real fact he was the man who held her heart.

August thought a moment. "They still haven't found who switched out the materials from the training," she stated.

He rubbed his chin along her hair. He'd heard something about the investigation but hadn't kept up with the details. Now he was glad Sol had. "That's a real shame. We lost a good officer that day."

"You know Swift Time could probably help."

"He probably could," Stx agreed. "Did it take you long to learn braille?"

She shrugged. "Not really. Reading the braille books to Isaac helps keep my skills sharp." She looked up at him. "You thinking of learning braille?"

"Might as well."

August shifted until she straddled his lap. He tensed as she cupped his face. "Relax," she told him. She reached for the sunglasses he wore.

He captured her hands before she could remove them.

"You don't have to hide from me," she said softly. "I already know what you look like."

"How?" he blurted before he could stop himself.

She chuckled. "Through touch."

He dropped his hands, and she removed his glasses. She folded the glasses, then placed them in Samson's shirt pocket.

August ran her fingers gently over his hair. The freshly cut fade prickled her fingers. She drifted over his forehead until she touched the jagged scar bisecting his left eyebrow.

She moved down to the lids that fluttered beneath her touch. Her lips followed with an even lighter touch.

Stx savored her touch, lifting his face so she could have as much access as she liked. He gripped her hips to hold her steady. He was aware of every breath and movement she made. Her scent, lavender mixed with something wholly female, tempted him. Had she always felt and smelled this good? He worked his fingers beneath the soft sweater she wore. Her skin was petal-soft, and he relished the velvet texture.

She brushed her lips against his in a barely-there kiss. His entire body went on point.

He gripped her hips a little tighter. He gripped a handful of her luscious derriere. It was firmer than he remembered. He ran his hands upward. Yes, she was definitely smaller than he remembered.

"You've lost weight."

"I have," she confirmed.

"Because of me?" Guilt gnawed at his insides.

She chuckled. "No, silly. Because of me." She grabbed his hand and guided it to her abdomen. "Feel that?" she pressed one of his fingers over a raised welt.

Not a welt. A scar. No more than two inches. Stx ran his fingers over the rest of Sol's stomach. There were four other lines in varying lengths. The smallest at a quarter-inch, the longest at two inches. "What happened?"

"Bariatric surgery," she confessed. "My health was getting out of control. I'd tried diets, exercising, pills, and losing a little of the weight, but it was not enough. When my doctor told me I was diabetic, it was time to get drastic."

"Oh, Sol."

She kissed him. "It was one of the best decisions I've ever made. I liked my body and curves before, but now I feel so much better and sexier and have more energy."

"That's why you don't eat a lot anymore," he mused.

She giggled. "Right."

She slid off his lap and pulled him to his feet. "C'mon, blind man. Let's see if you still got moves."

For the first time in several months, Stx woke warm and satisfied. He snuggled deeper into the super-soft sheets and inhaled the sweet scent of lavender, vanilla, and musk. Their combined scents. He snaked a hand across the sheets reaching for his woman. He wanted to see her and kiss her awake.

What he got was his phone. He snapped open his eyes. Nothing.

Stx fell back against the pillows with a sigh. There was always that disorienting moment where he thought he had sight. He clutched the phone to his bare chest.

"You have one audio message," the voice announced.

Stx followed the prompts to listen to the message. A broad grin spread his face as he listened to Sol's voice.

"Good morning, Samson. I hope you don't mind, but I'm wearing my ring again. I left breakfast in the microwave for you. I'll call you when I'm done with my coffee date."

"Coffee date?" he muttered. Oh right, she was having coffee with one of her students. The man who'd pulled her from the training center. He kicked off the sheets and stood. Again, he took a moment to bring Sol's room to memory before following the bed around to an open area. A few more feet and he entered the en suite bathroom.

This house was as familiar to him as his own. Once showered and dressed, Stx took a few minutes to explore the house. So different and so similar without sight.

He marveled at the texture of the fireplace. Rough brick for the face and the cool gritty texture of the grout. The scent of burnt wood clung to the air. He sniffed appreciatively. He moved out from the fireplace, his right hand grazing the chair he had tossed his jacket over last night. He ran his hand over the back, but the jacket wasn't there. Sol hung it up. But his cane was balanced neatly on the seam of the cushion.

He touched the cane beneath his arm. His toes brushed the area rug as he crossed to the leather sofa. Behind the sofa was another table. Here a bowl of fruit combined with the scent from the fireplace. How had he not noticed the fragrances before?

He followed the sofa table to the sliding patio doors. The vertical blinds click-clacked as he ran his fingers against them. Next came the wall of the dining room. He used it to get him to the far side of the dining room. He reached out a left hand and felt for the back of the rounded chair. Now that he knew the table, the stools to the bar were right in front of him. The surface was spotless.

He set his cane on the countertop and followed it around to the kitchen. He'd admired her kitchen before, but now he had a greater appreciation for her organization.

He found the microwave, then had a moment of panic when there were no bump dots. Then he remembered that Sol's home was automated. All he had to do was tell the microwave what setting and for how long.

Satisfied at achieving yet another accomplishment, Stx settled in at the bar to enjoy his hot breakfast and coffee when his phone rang.

"You're actually answering your phone," Potter said.

"What do you want, Potter?" Stx never liked the cop, but maybe there was information on what happened.

"We've been working on this, and I can't let it go. I found some prints on the bomb fragments that matched some prints we took from the various sites."

"Oh?"

"The thing is that only the person who made the bomb could've put them there. So I went back to the first few scenes, and the prints were there as well."

"So you found a match."

"Yes, but it struck me as odd because we'd dismissed the prints because they were in the building that day."

"Is there more?" Stx pushed.

"Maybe, but I wanted to give you that update and let you know you're not forgotten."

Stx set down his phone, his mind racing. Who had been at the earlier sites? Who with access to bomb materials could have wanted to take out the bomb squad?

August sipped her mocha latte. Around her, the whir of blenders, hiss of frothers, and amiable chatter filled the coffeehouse.

"I know it's been a long time coming, but I truly appreciate you stopping me from opening that package," August began. "I shudder to think what would've happened if you hadn't been there."

"You know I got your back, Sol," David said. "I'd do any-thing for you."

There it was again. He was exuding far too much emo-tion for a simple thank you.

"Did you want a pastry? I remember how you like their double chocolate brownies," he offered. "I could get you one to go if you like."

"No. No. I'm good," she said quickly. "I really wanted to give you a little time and thank you."

"I love you, and I'll do anything to make you my woman." He rushed the last part. "You deserve so much better than a gigolo."

Stunned, Sol sat back. Did he profess his love for her? Oh, burnt beans. This was a dill pickle she didn't like at all. She moistened her dry lips and prepared to deliver an easy letdown.

"I had no idea you felt that way about me," she stated truthfully. Honesty was good, right?

Fabric rustled, and David clasped her hands in his. As gently as she could, she removed her hands from his.

"I've wanted to tell you for so long," he said. "Ever since I've been coming to your training center, you've made me want to do better. You motivate me when nothing else has," he gushed. "You got Misty, well, perfect. She's a model dog now. I've started working out and everything."

Goodness, this was harder than she thought. "Those are all wonderful reasons, David, but I'm not in love with you. I love someone else."

"He's a gigolo!" David spat. "He makes a habit of messing with women's hearts then betraying them. Don't you know that? He did the same thing to my sister, but I showed him."

August set her cup down and reached for the leash beneath her left thigh. "I need to get to work," she said. She stood, and Riley came to life with a vigorous shake and a jangle of tags.

"I'm sorry. I'm so excited to have this time with you that I lost my head." David stood, scraping the chair against the floor. "I didn't mean no harm."

August touched his sleeve. "I'm flattered you love me, but I do not feel the same about you," she stated. "You're a good man, but I'm not in love with you. I'm sorry."

"But I want to be with you," he pleaded.

August grasped the handle of the harness. "Forward, find the door out," she told Riley. "I'm sorry, David. We can only be friends."

As fast as Riley walked, she willed him to go faster. She had been flattered by David's admission, but there couldn't be more between them than there was now. And if he persisted in pursuing her, she'd have to drop him as a client. It would be best if she terminated their relationship now. Other dog trainers in the city were just as good, if not better.

Riley paused. Sol placed a hand on his head and followed him to the door. "Good boy!" she praised and pushed into the cold.

It was cold and freezing rain. Sol sighed at the sensation of another typical winter in beautiful Ann Arbor. She steered to the sidewalk and caught movement. A moment later, she was covered from the rain.

"I saw you get up," a friendly male voice explained.

"Oh, Jeff. Thanks." She couldn't quite keep the relief from her voice. Jeff often drove her to last-minute appointments. "You being here is really appreciated."

"Not a problem. The car is just right here."

He led her a few feet away and opened the back passenger door. Sol quickly unharnessed Riley, then slid into the leather seat. Riley curled in the footwell. Once she was inside, Jeff closed the door and entered the driver's seat.

"Warm enough?" he asked, clicking his seatbelt.

"Yes." She settled back against the seat, chewing the inside of her lip. She had to let Samson know how coffee went this morning. She wondered if he'd found everything okay.

"Hey," August greeted when Samson answered the phone some eighteen minutes later.

"How was coffee?" he asked.

"Interesting and creepy," she replied. She ran through the highlights of what happened.

"What did you say this guy's name was?"

"David um Marsh, I think. I'd have to check my files again, but he's been coming to the training center for the last year or so."

"Well, the man has good taste in women." Samson's grin came through loud and clear.

"I never even knew the guy was interested in me." August filled the dog bowls with food. There was only Coco and a border collie in the kennels. "When I told him I didn't feel the same way about him and was in love with someone else, he started ranting about the man being a gigolo." She waited a beat. "Is there something you want to tell me about your personal life?"

He laughed. "I have never slept with a woman for money or fine things. Although, there's a first time for everything. Are you volunteering to be my sugar mama?"

Hot tears filled her eyes. She blinked them away. It was so good to have Samson joking again. She'd missed his humor the most.

"How about I meet you at the training center with lunch?" Samson offered. "It's only fair since you made me dinner and breakfast."

She grinned. "That sounds like a plan." August disconnected the call and dropped the phone in her pocket. She squinted toward one corner of the office where Riley gnawed what had once been a bone. Walking around the counter, she made sure the front door was locked. She didn't want anyone coming in while she was out back with the dogs. Besides, she wasn't open yet.

With the dogs fed and watered, August went through some obedience training. Coco, the little terrier, was a treat. The little dog pranced around in excitement. August held a treat for her to eat. The dog daintily took the little biscuit and ran back to her kennel.

August laughed and held a bigger biscuit out to the border collie. The big shaggy dog sniffed at the treat.

"C'mon, boy, I won't hurt you," she crooned. "Obviously, you know the commands, so you got the training. But then someone didn't take care of you." She continued to hold out the treat.

Cautiously the dog inched forward. As soon as he had the biscuit in his mouth, he turned and ran away.

"Poor thing."

The border collie came in as a rescue four months ago. Sol wasn't sure the dog could be saved. It had lost most of its fur and was so emaciated that it spent a week healing in the vet's office. Somehow, the sweet dog pulled through but was still skittish about taking food from August's hand.

August set the gate so the dogs wouldn't get out, then returned to the front to unlock the door. It was time to start classes.

⌒

Stx sat in front of his laptop. There was something he needed to do. Something he hadn't done since he woke up in the hospital. Taking a breath, he opened his web browser and typed in Emerald Foster. The computerized voice announced every keystroke. He hadn't read Emerald's obituary. It took a little doing, but he finally found it.

He listened as it listed her parents; both died when she turned 16. The obituary listed a couple of siblings, one older and one younger. Her older brother raised his two younger siblings, David and Janica. It went on to list Emerald's education, her years of service with the department, and all her commendations.

Stx wiggled the mouse. What had he heard? He tried to get back to the part about her family and couldn't remember how to make the computer read from the beginning, but he did figure out how to maneuver the up and down keys on the keyboard to make the computer read line by line.

The first name could be a coincidence. Stx sat back, trying to remember if Emerald had ever said her brother's first name. Shaking his head, he picked up his cell. There was nothing wrong with wanting to be sure.

Chapter Thirteen

August shrugged into her jacket before she grabbed Riley's leash. It was almost time for lunch, and she hadn't taken her dog out since she arrived that morning. He nudged the leash, trying to thread his head through the loop. She chuckled. "That's not how this one goes, you big goof." She clipped the leash to his collar and headed out the back door.

A cold wind slapped her in the face. She turned her back with a muffled shriek. "It's too cold for this," she griped. Riley dipped and sniffed as if he enjoyed the cold. "You don't have to rub in the fact you have a fur coat."

She led him, or rather he tugged her to a spot of patchy snow where he circled, sniffed, then walked away. He repeated this twice more before he settled on a spot.

August caught a glimpse of his tail curved and low to the ground. She readied a poop bag over her hand and ran it down the dog's curved spine in the shape of a C until she got to the bottom. When Riley moved away, August picked up his hot and steaming poop.

Footsteps crunched behind her. Before she could call out, someone grabbed her from behind. August screamed. One strong arm curled around her waist and lifted her.

What could she do? She had to get away. Poop still warmed her right hand. Moving her head as far right as she could, she shoved the feces in her assailant's face.

The scream pierced the winter air. Stx's heart hammered as he turned in the direction of the scream. "That was Sol," he told his driver.

Sol screamed again.

"Hurry. Something's wrong."

Arms outstretched, Stx ran. He had the fleeting thought that this was the stupidest thing he could possibly do, but Sol was in trouble. No one screams like that for fun. And blast it all, he couldn't see. But he could hear scuffling as if two people were struggling.

A dog panted, and another growled.

"Ugh!"

"Ow!"

"You bitch!"

Stx had the voice now, and he ran full tilt into a heavy body. Both went crashing to the frozen cement. Stx applied elbows and fists until the man stopped moving

"Sol?" Stx jumped to his feet, turning in a circle. "Sol!"

"Here." Footsteps crunched, and a hand grasped his. He pulled Sol close. "Oh my gosh, are you okay?"

Her head moved against his chest. "He—he grabbed me."

Stx became aware of an earthy odor and wrinkled his nose. There was something smeared on his coat and hands, and Sol also had some on her. "What's that smell?"

Humor filled her voice. "I shoved poop in his face."

Stx threw back his head and laughed. "Very resourceful."

One Week Later

Stx smiled. There was quite a crowd in here tonight. He could hear the difference. Voices bounced and mingled with laughter. The last time he'd taken the stage was after seeing Sol after so many years. Now he was going to take the stage with her.

"Nervous?" he said in her ear.

"Are you kidding? I'm too excited to be nervous," she answered.

"You got this!" Johnny said.

Stx glowed with pride and contentment. Finally, Sol was a part of his band. He reached out and gripped her hand. She squeezed back. "Well, I'm nervous," he admitted.

And he wasn't saying that to make her feel better. Even though they'd spent the last week practicing, he was still unsure about some of the cues.

Johnny slapped him on the back. "Stop worrying. The last time we played, and she was in the room, you dropped a stick and missed a few beats."

Stx laughed. That happened because he'd spied Sol dancing on the dance floor. "Well there won't be a pretty woman on the dance floor to tempt me," he quipped.

Sol laughed. "Is that why you lost your stick?"

"Yeah," he said, wrapping an arm around her waist.

A week ago, he would never have thought they'd be sharing the same stage. A week ago, he could've lost Sol to an overzealous man.

David Marsh Foster confessed to sending the confetti bombs. He was hoping to use the bombs as a way to curry favor and love from Sol. When David learned Sol was interested in Stx and that Stx was his sister Emerald's partner, David conspired to get rid of Stx. Only Emerald tried to intervene.

"C'mon, let's get you settled on the drums," Johnny said, nudging Stx forward.

Stx leaned over and kissed Sol. "You make me so happy."

Sol pinched his butt, and he chuckled. He sat behind the drums. He thought the opening song was appropriate for them. Keisha Cole's "Make me Over."

Later that evening, Stx and August sat on the sofa in front of a roaring fire. "You were magnificent tonight," Stx praised.

She wrapped her arms around him. "So were you."

Leaning into her embrace, he kissed her. "You think we can make out in front of the fire and not get interrupted?" He trailed kisses from her jawline to the vee of her shirt.

"I'm daring, but not that daring. The little guy is liable to walk in on us." She shifted on the cushions until Stx was settled between her thighs.

Heat singed his erection, and he ground against her. "Then I think we need to take this to the bedroom," he said huskily. He stood, offering her his hand. As he pulled her to her feet, a knock reverberated on the door.

"Who could that be?" Stx demanded.

"Anyone knocking at this hour never brings good news."

They walked down the hall together. "Yes?" Stx pressed the button for the intercom.

"Stx. It's Falls."

August stepped back as Stx unlocked and opened the door. Cold blasted them. Falls came in and quickly closed the door. "I'm sorry to disturb you so late, but this can't wait."

"What is it?" Stx demanded.

"David Foster, Rodney Kimball, and one other prisoner have escaped."

Author Bio

Lynn Chantale, a romance novelist, short story writer, and part-time background singer, has published many stories across several genres. Her works include *Sex, Lies, and Joysticks, True Detective Series,* and *Broken Lens* to name a few.

When she's not actively planning world domination, she's dominating her household, family, and her cat Shakespeare. You can visit her at any of her cyber haunts:

Website: https://www.thehouseoflynn.com

Twitter: https://twitter.com/lynnchantale

Facebook: https://www.facebook.com/LynnChantale Author

Facebook Group Tale's Tells: https://www.facebook.com/groups/talestells

Instagram: https://www.instagram.com/lynn_chantale/

Youtube: https://www.youtube.com/channel/UCHbA ParOHDB7cwfSwUtU3cA